OF PA

HEIDI STONE

CHIMERA

Of Pain and Delight first published in 2000 by
Chimera Publishing Ltd
PO Box 152
Waterlooville
Hants
PO8 9FS

Printed and bound in Great Britain by
Omnia Books Ltd Glasgow

This book is sold subject to the condition that it shall not, by way of trade or otherwise, be lent, resold, hired out or otherwise circulated without the publisher's prior written consent in any form of binding or cover other than that in which it is published, and without a similar condition being imposed on the subsequent purchaser.

The characters and situations in this book are entirely imaginary and bear no relation to any real person or actual happening.

Copyright © Heidi Stone

The right of Heidi Stone to be identified as author of this book has been asserted in accordance with section 77 and 78 of the Copyrights Designs and Patents Act 1988

OF PAIN AND DELIGHT

Heidi Stone

This novel is fiction – in real life practice safe sex

'Such a fine arse,' the evil man muttered, as though to some unseen audience. 'It would seem a shame to mark such perfect globes.'

'Then why mark them?' Sahria said slowly. 'Why not continue to enjoy them as you have been doing, with your hands and your tongue?' Shackled as she was, she found the idea quite entertaining, although the very thought of allowing the repulsive man to do anything more intimate than she had just suggested was quite out of the question.

'Silence, vixen,' he commanded, his tone reminding her that she had little choice in the matter.

Chapter One

The first sensation that Sahria experienced as she slipped from her fitful sleep into a dim world of reality was a dull ache between her legs.

It was not unpleasant – in fact, it was instead a rather warm memory of recent and pleasurable intrusion. She tried to move her hand downward to touch herself intimately, not to relieve the gentle pain but to relax her rapidly awakening feelings of desire with an erotic caress. To her surprise she found that she was unable to move.

She opened her eyes and arched her neck to look up and behind. She could now see that her arms were stretched above her head with the wrists securely bound by unforgiving leather straps. She struggled a little and suddenly winced as a sharp stab of pain spiked through her right nipple, which forced her into full consciousness. The wooden bench felt hard against her naked back and the rough surface chafed against the softness of her plump but firm buttocks.

Surprisingly, Sahria found the sensation to be somewhat pleasurable, despite the fact that there were no cushions or sheets to offer her any comfort, just the bare, unyielding base. She moved her bottom against the harsh wood, taking care not to encourage splinters to penetrate her skin. Her flesh was sore. It was as though she had been recently spanked, caned or whipped, and yet she had no memory of such recent delights. She struggled to remember the previous days or even hours, but her mind remained a fog of uncertainty.

The aching need for satisfaction that throbbed between her splayed legs was becoming too much to bear. Years of habitually sating herself with probing fingertips upon waking were taking their toll. She began to imagine the sight of her clitoris, clearly visible to anybody who may wish to view her current naked vulnerability. The thought of hidden eyes watching her thrilled her immensely.

She raised her head and glanced down her bound length as her eyes slowly became accustomed to the half-light. A fine but visibly strong chain was linked to the gold of her nipple ring, with the other end securely fastened somewhere beneath the crude bed. A similar chain tugged fiercely at her other nipple. Normally, her large breasts would proudly thrust upwards when she lay flat, but the tightness of the chains caused them instead to be pulled firmly apart.

Sahria tugged at the chains at her wrists again in the hope of making them give, but the pain was too acute. Frustrated and becoming increasingly angry, she lay her head back on the solid surface, her brow covered in perspiration. Gradually, her thoughts became less and less confused and memories of the night before began to seep back to her.

They had done this to her!

Sahria hissed audibly through clenched teeth as she recalled how the vermin had subjugated her in this way, and hatred seethed through her brain. They would pay, she vowed. They would pay dearly for their impertinence.

She raised her head again in order to look down at her lower body and legs. She saw immediately that her ankles were tightly strapped with leather bonds, pulling her limbs wide apart in the most obscene fashion. A second pair of finely linked chains had been secured to two of the tiny gold rings with which she had once so proudly pierced the outer lips of her sex. The effect of the chains was to pull the succulent flesh apart to reveal her inner dampness to the damp air of her prison. She sensed a sliver of her juice slipping from within her body to slide sensuously between her buttocks. She was uncomfortable, but at the same time incongruously aroused. She badly needed sexual release, but she was also very, very angry.

Sahria reflected on how the two black slaves had suddenly turned on her as she played her games of subjugation with them. They almost smothered her with their giant but normally suppliant bodies, and they took her as they wished, penetrating her in every conceivable and erotic fashion and bringing her over and over again to shattering climax.

But the sensations of orgasm had, if anything, only served to sharpen her fury.

How dare they?

How dare mere slaves pleasure themselves with their princess?

She remembered spitting venomously at them as she struggled, and yet the more they fought with her, the more they held her down, the more she wanted them inside her. Their sizes were magnificent. Their huge, ebony cocks had filled her oiled pussy and her mouth at will, never relaxing for a moment as though repaying her for years of physical and mental torment.

Yes, she thought, she would make them pay.

Sahria raised her bottom slightly from the splintered wood and the chains tugged on her labia. The feeling was nevertheless pleasurable, like the urgent caress of an ardent lover opening her to the gaze of any unseen eyes that may be watching. She rotated her hips slowly. The sharp stabs of pain between her legs became as delightful to her as a fluttering tongue against the oozing lips of her cunt. She raised her back as much as she could. The searing pain in her nipples thrilled her in a way she could never have imagined before. Her pussy throbbed and her juices seemed to be seeping from her body to soak the hard wood beneath her. She pushed her hips upwards. The lower set of chains grabbed ferociously at her tender sex flesh and pulled the lips even wider apart. She suddenly felt the muscles of her groin constricting and, with virtually no warning she came with a loud and desperate squeal. The pain was almost unbearable but the more it hurt the more she fought against her pleasurable restraints. Never in her young life had she experienced such a violent and shattering orgasm. She gasped for air, her hips writhing and her flesh feeling as if it was about to be torn apart.

Slowly, her breathing became more controlled. She relaxed and allowed her mind to wander as the blood thumped heavily through her tortured body.

Her lascivious needs satisfied for the moment, she allowed her thoughts to travel back to her childhood and she remembered how her father, the king, had taught her of her superiority to the thousands of peasants who lived in the city, and of her divine right to force them into obeying her will lest they suffer the penalty. Gleefully, she would order the servants of the royal household to perform the most embarrassing and demeaning of tasks. The walls of the palace echoed to the sounds of her childish laughter as they accepted her volition, their expressions of compliance undoubtedly concealing seething hatred, but above all, their fear.

She came to savour – nay *need* – the fear. Often, when a particular prank had gone really well, she would imagine that she could actually smell the terror of the poor wretches under her control, and possibly even taste it on their sweating flesh.

Al-Fahoud, her esteemed father, would nightly be entertained by her excesses, and he clapped and cheered loudly as her victims crawled, snivelling from the room and grovelling in total subservience. As the child grew into a woman her beauty became legendary, as did her reputation for cruelty.

She was exceptionally tall for a woman of the time, close to six-foot, and her height was often accentuated by the high heels she preferred to wear. Her legs were long and lithe and had circled about the waist of many a lover, her heels digging into manly, thrusting buttocks. Her own firm globes were perfectly rounded and jutted back in a pert and inviting fashion while her hips curved delightfully to form her narrow waist. Her navel was invariably adorned with a single ruby, and above it her breasts rose majestically, graced by

9

proud nipples that she had recently taken to piercing with gold rings.

To say her face was beautiful would have been a gross understatement. Her flawless features were such that they could charm the strongest willed man into abject submission. Her wonderful countenance was framed by tresses of long black hair, the sheen of which shone as though with a florescence of its own. Her hair cascaded all the way down to the small of her back and brushed lightly against the upturned swell of her buttocks, as if guiding the eye of the beholder to her most intimate of delights.

Often, she would parade around the court naked, save for high-heeled leather boots that covered virtually all of her legs and thighs, in the full knowledge that the men would be lusting after her, yet unable to show their desire for fear of severe punishment.

Sometimes she would link her nipple rings with a thin gold chain and later, after she had courageously pierced the lips of her succulent pussy with yet more rings, she wore more chains attached to them, fashioning them to traverse her body in the most erotic manner to emphasise the smooth lines and delicate curves of her superb body.

The kingdom was rich and her father was immensely wealthy. Lords and princes travelled from all parts of the known world to court his beautiful daughter, only to find themselves helpless in her mastery and becoming as much her vassals as the lowliest of her subjects.

But still they came, despite tales of her excesses

told by travellers and merchants, and still they suffered. They did so willingly, totally enslaved by her beauty and graceful charms, that conquered their wills while her angelic features clouded the judgement and good sense of the most intelligent of men.

Only once did she let her guard down. Only once did it seem that the princess of pleasure and domination was to be subdued. There was talk of little else in the teeming market places throughout the kingdom for many months.

He had arrived alone, without even a slave or bearer accompanying him as he walked purposefully into the court. Announced as Prince Sarne of Persia he strode confidently, almost arrogantly towards the throne, his head unbowed and his steely gaze fixed firmly on the sight of the lovely princess who sat at her father's feet. Al-Fahoud had been quick to show his anger.

'Know you not that you must prostrate yourself at the feet of the king?' he bellowed, his face red and twisted with rage.

'Were I the type to do so, my lord,' the prince answered in a calm and unwavering tone of voice, 'then I would not be a worthy consort for your daughter, the Princess Sahria.' He bowed towards her, a conceited smile playing across his lips.

She looked up at him, her deep brown eyes reflected in his stare. There was lust in his gaze but there was also more – much more.

His expression showed strength of purpose and forcefulness that she had not seen in a man before, and she knew then that she wanted him. She knew she wanted to control his will and force him to beg for

11

the pain and pleasure that she was fully confident only she could inflict upon him. Although barely eighteen years of age, she had learnt much from her father, building constantly on his instruction and advice thanks to her own unbridled imagination.

The Princess Sahria had decided there and then that this prince of Persia would be hers, and he would beg.

Al-Fahoud rose from his throne, the look on his face throwing the assembled multitude of courtiers into visible spasms of terror. They knew that this arrogant Persian was about to die, there, in the courtroom, and that his blood was to spill onto the highly polished marble floor.

Sahria recognised her father's ire immediately and stood up next to him. She took his arm and whispered to him quickly before he could take up his sword and slay the intruder, which was clearly his intention.

'Stay, father,' she hissed, gripping his arm tightly. 'He intrigues me. Let me deal with this upstart in my own way.' She grinned and licked her top lip suggestively. The old man's stern features calmed and a trace of a smile appeared at the corners of his cruel mouth.

'What would you do with him, daughter?' he asked with a wicked leer.

'Trust me, father,' Sahria whispered, glad that his temper had subsided as rapidly as it had risen. 'He will know pleasure but, oh, he will know pain, and he will beg for it.'

Al-Fahoud nodded in agreement, knowing his daughter was well versed in such matters. He sat down again and smirked contentedly. 'My daughter wishes to consort with you, although why, I cannot imagine. You have until the dawning of tomorrow to plead with her.'

Sahria smiled and kissed her father lightly on the cheek. The old man immediately pulled away from her in disgust at this unprecedented show of affection from his daughter. Nevertheless, he watched with a broad grin as Sahria took the arm of the stranger and led him from the throne room.

'And may Allah protect your soul, good prince,' he was heard to mutter.

Princess Sahria led Prince Sarne to her chambers, gripping his strong arm with an excessive tightness that would have made lesser men wince. His gait remained confident and his expression stayed cool and aloof. She wondered at this man – could she have at last met her match?

She took him quickly through her boudoir and directly into her bedchamber, angrily dismissing her handmaidens with a flourish of her free arm. The timid women scuttled out of her presence like frightened mice, although they all took a moment to glance enviously at the perfect features of her handsome companion.

Sahria closed the heavy door noisily, barring it securely.

'We will be together until the dawn,' she announced, standing immediately in front of him with her eyes fixed coldly on his. 'And, by the time the sun has warmed the old stones of this palace you will be my slave.'

13

Prince Sarne shook his head contemptuously. 'Not so, princess,' he said, his tone if anything stronger, and his attitude more arrogant than before. 'It is *you* who will submit and it is you who will beg. I know of your reputation and I am fully aware that you are used to compliance in men... but not this time.'

Sahria laughed and turned away from him contemptuously. She tossed back her head, the long black tresses of her hair brushing lightly against her pert buttocks, their charms hidden from the prince's gaze only by the sheerest of silk. 'And what magic?' she said with a sneer. 'What wondrous power do you posses that gives you so much strength of will that you dare attempt to control one such as I?'

'I know many tricks,' he replied. 'I am well versed in such matters. But most of all, I have this!' Sarne threw back his cloak in one practised movement and stood proudly before her. She gasped. He was naked, his olive-skinned physique glowing with a subtle sheen in the soft light of the evening. There was barely a trace of hair on his body apart from the dark, luxuriant curls that framed his proud features, and a small bush of thick fuzz at his crotch. His penis stood hard and erect, pointing like a fearsome spear at her sudden frailness. Its size was immense, not unlike the images portrayed within the erotic icons in the temple that she had savoured in her solitary moments, sights that had filled her nights with dreams of future delights. Now such a vision appeared before her, and it was real and menacing in the extreme. Never had she dreamt that a mortal man could posses such a weapon!

The thing seemed to be regarding her through the

single eye set in its angry purple head, as though scrutinising her with disdain. The heavily veined stem bore a length similar to that of her own forearm and its girth, if anything, was more than that of her slender wrist. She sensed her will deserting her the longer she gazed at the monster, her arms falling limply to her sides and her eyes widening with desire.

Princess Sahria knew at that moment that her ultimate desire was to absorb every part of that magnificent cock within her loins. She knew it might hurt, at least until her body became used to the sheer size of the prince's wondrous rod, and that the massive head of the thing would beat mercilessly against the deepest regions of her soaking honeypot.

But she also knew that she must have him.

'Well, my princess,' he said, as he gripped his cock firmly at the root to force the devil to even more immensity, 'who is to be lord and master tonight?'

Sahria said nothing. Instead, she fell to her knees at his feet and took the hard stalk in her hand with a gentleness that was all too uncommon in her. She stared in wonder at the gnarled pole, astounded that her fingers could barely encircle its girth. She leant forward and kissed the bulbous head, before running her tongue around the thick knob and then finally taking him within the silky sheath of her young mouth.

Suddenly he pulled from her heavenly grasp, his penis waving like a triumphant flagpole at the scene of a battle and, grasping his cloak around his body he swiftly unbarred the door and threw it open. 'Princess,' he announced firmly, 'there can be no greater cruelty than denial, and I have denied you the feel of my weapon within your loins tonight. One day I will return. You will not know when, but on that day I will conquer you and abuse you into spasms of total ecstasy that you will never have dreamt possible. For now, you may have the last sight of that which will impale you, to fill your visions until my return.'

So saying, the Prince of Persia once more drew back his cloak and allowed his penis to thrust into the open. Sahria tried to fight her desire to stare at it, not wishing to appear weak, but the temptation was too great and she couldn't resist quickly glancing at the proffered prize. She swallowed hard, his intimate taste still on her lips.

Sarne covered himself again with a flourish and left the room, pushing past the handmaidens who returned to stare in astonishment at the sight of their vicious mistress, kneeling, her eyes glazed and her trembling body racked with lust.

Princess Sahria sighed to herself as she remembered the event, then threw her head to one side in anger. A year had passed since that time, during which she had vented her fury and frustrations in ever more salacious pursuits, but she never either forgot or forgave Prince Sarne of Persia. Her exasperation filled the palace so that even Al-Fahoud himself lived in fear of her rage, and kept well out of her way. Tales of her lascivious acts spread throughout the country. The men – and indeed the women – lived lives of paradox; extreme fear mingled with an intense desire to sample the delights and mysteries of the court of the princess of pleasure. Many, very many, were to be successful.

What little light chose to creep into her dank prison through the tiny barred window was fading fast. Although time was beginning to have little meaning for her, Sahria felt it was too soon for night to embrace the cold walls of the palace with its silent shroud. A storm must be imminent, she thought, the heavens preparing to unleash their fury upon the mortals below with an anger that could, nevertheless, scarcely match her own. She liked the storms, the ferocious blasts of power engulfing all unfortunate enough to be without shelter. In happier times she would have rushed out into the rain, naked, offering herself to the sheer power and seeking to sate herself within the energy to soak up its strength.

Not this time.

As the first flash of lightning seared its white light across her vision she struggled against her bonds. The tightness of the leather around her wrists and ankles gripped her unforgivingly and the pain in her nipples and labia became intense as the thin slivers of chain tugged her tender flesh mercilessly. She cursed loudly. Oh, how the pathetic animals would suffer!

The thunder crashed as if to echo her anger and then roared into the distance like a wounded beast.

The lightning flashed again, this time much brighter than before. Sahria closed her eyes and gritted her teeth in frustration. She strained against her bonds and experienced a brief feeling of incongruous delight at her vulnerable state. She moved again and felt a sharp pain between her splayed legs. A sense of total defencelessness sent a wave of pleasure coursing through her body. She thrust her hips upward

17

purposely, and the pain stabbed the soaking lips of her pussy as her movements caused the chains to wrench them further apart. The agony thrilled her but quickly became too much to bear, and she relaxed her body once more.

She allowed her mind to wander again and, for some reason she began to recall memories of the time when she had witnessed the subjugation of Calema, her lovely young friend. She remembered just how much she had enjoyed the spectacle; little knowing that one day she would find herself in a similar defenceless position.

She smiled to herself as she recalled how Calema, then barely seventeen and still a virgin, had stood trembling while three handmaidens stripped and oiled her delicate body to prepare her for what was to come. Calema had looked pleadingly at Sahria, but her response was merely to laugh as one of the servants slipped three fingers between the girl's shaven sex lips and took her maidenhead with a swift, practised movement.

Calema made no sound, although she was trembling visibly. The dampness between her legs had become very apparent; her open pussy lips glinting like the dew-covered petals of a tiny pink rose. She would have known there was no stopping the ceremony now, and it was clear that she didn't want to, despite her unmistakable terror.

Sahria clapped her hands and the girl was blindfolded and then led to a small raised platform in the centre of the room. At each corner was bolted a length of thick chain fixed with manacles, their purpose clear. A wooden frame in the shape of an inverted U stood in the middle of the dais, the apex covered with padded cloth that served to protect Calema's stomach as she was made to bend over the construction, her wrists and ankles then shackled firmly to the unyielding chains.

So restrained, she waited, the long tresses of her golden-blonde hair cascading from her bowed head to touch the floor, and her legs held straight and parted so that the sight of her tiny bottom was presented for the assembled company to enjoy. For what must have seemed like an eternity to the hapless virgin the people stood, watching her as she trembled in fearful anticipation, the only sound being that of her quiet, gentle sobbing.

Sahria knew her friend's tears were not from fear, but caused by arousal. Delightful interludes with her in the recent past, when their curious fingers had pleasured and probed each other was proof enough of that. The sobs were very similar to the sounds Calema made following orgasm.

Sahria clapped her hands again and Calema raised her head as best as she could, startled. The Grand Vizier stepped forward, for it was to be he who would have the honour of taking the young girl's virginity. He ran his hands over the small, firm buttocks, caressing them lovingly. Leaning forward, he planted a wet kiss between them and then ran his tongue down to her forbidden orifice. He lingered there, licking hungrily at the puckered little hole for longer than Sahria felt was necessary, but Calema didn't seem to mind if her soft moans of pleasure were to be believed.

Eventually, however, he moved to press his tongue firmly against the softness of her unsullied sex, the lips of which were already soaked with her juices and the oils administered by the handmaidens.

She groaned as he licked her there, her buttocks stiffening and her breathing becoming laboured. Expertly, the Vizier's tongue lapped and suckled at the offered prize, the tip flicking incessantly over the hard bud of her clitoris as he pushed three, then four fingers inside her warmth. She shuddered as he moved his hand up and down, and then sighed with notable disappointment when he moved it away from her.

'I sense that your friend is ready, mistress,' the Vizier said as he removed his cloak. Sahria stepped forward and bent to closely examine the girl's sex. She stroked the lips with her fingertips.

'She's very wet,' she agreed. 'It will take quite a man to fill her!'

The Grand Vizier moved forward, now fully naked and with his erection held long and proud before him. Sahria reached out and caught hold of it, then put it to her mouth and engulfed the head with her pouting lips. She felt him throb and tasted the salty evidence of his arousal. Anxious that he should perform the required task, she took him from her mouth and put the end of his cock to the wet sex lips so blatantly displayed for all to see.

Calema tensed and began to cry. 'Please, princess,' she sobbed. 'Please beg him to be gentle. I am frightened.'

Sahria kissed her young friend's bottom lightly and, gripping the thick cock firmly by the root, moved it slowly so that the swollen head slid sensuously over the outer lips of Calema's pussy. 'Relax, sweet child,' she soothed. 'You are more than capable of accommodating this fine weapon and, when it fills you your cries will be ones of joy and ecstasy!'

She directed the lust-engorged end of the Vizier's stalk to the waiting opening and licked her lips as it slid cautiously inside – three, four, and then five inches before stopping for a moment.

'Please, princess,' Calema begged. 'Please, it hurts… it is too big!'

'Relax, my precious. Relax and it will be much easier for you.'

Calema must have heeded her advice because four or five more inches slid quickly inside her tight sheath, until the Vizier's belly became pressed hard against the soft globes of her bottom. Sahria moved around the prone figure of her friend and took off the blindfold. She kissed her lightly on the lips. 'How does it feel now?'

'It is strangely wonderful,' the girl mewed. 'The pain is gone, and I feel so full inside my loins.'

Sahria stood up, grinning cruelly. 'Now, Grand Vizier,' she barked, 'fuck her! Fuck her hard until you lose your seed within her! When that happens your fine cock will be replaced by another, and then another, until Calema knows the true meaning of pleasurable agony!'

The Vizier obeyed immediately, hammering his long cock in and out of the frail young body set so delicately at his mercy. Calema raised her head and looked round with fear in her eyes. There were many men, some of them already displaying fine erections, anxiously waiting to take their turn to impale her. She looked again at Sahria with tears in her eyes, but the princess at once detected the flush of total arousal in her facial expression and knew that her job was done.

The ceremony lasted well into the night. Calema, once a precious flower of virginity happily accepted most, if not all of the host of young men who vied with each other to be the next to sate themselves within her welcoming vulnerability.

Calema changed little since that day; her reputation exceeded only by that of the princess herself. She was keen to learn and Sahria was always only too pleased to instruct her in the many pleasures and diversions to which she herself had become adept. Her young charge had also developed her own preferences, of course, and would often regale Sahria with lurid accounts of her many sexual escapades.

Unlike Sahria, however, Calema seemed to prefer to be dominated by her lovers, albeit by her own design. She also often demanded anonymity of those who would take her, insisting that their heads be masked and their voices be silent. Sahria didn't consider such ideas to be repulsive, of course, and often enjoyed the erotic spectacle of seeing her young friend tied up on a bed or lashed to a fucking-frame while numerous hooded but otherwise naked men queued to use and abuse her.

It seemed odd to her that she now found herself in a similar situation to that so frequently enjoyed by her friend. The ache between her legs was now entirely caused by rampant desire, and mental images of

Calema lying prostrate and chained whilst her lithe body was plundered by some nameless hulk didn't help to ease her pain in the slightest.

She suddenly began to wonder if her friend was safe. Would she be likewise restrained, perhaps in another prison somewhere within the rambling passageways of the old palace? Perhaps her fate had been worse, far worse. There had been the distinct noise of battle resounding from outside during the long hours that the two slaves had taken Sahria, but the intense pleasure she was experiencing at the time had caused her to blot out the sounds.

The iron door to the dungeon opened with a resounding thud. Princess Sahria raised her head as far as her bonds would allow and saw the large silhouette of a man standing in the arched portal. 'Well, sweet princess,' boomed a voice she instantly recognised. 'We meet again.'

'Sarne!' she hissed venomously. 'Are you responsible for this?'

The figure moved forward, the dim torchlight catching his proud features and highlighting the cruelty of his expression. 'I vowed I would return,' he growled, 'and now your kingdom is mine.'

Sahria felt a tightness within her chest as the enormity of his words hit her. 'What do you mean?' she demanded. 'Where is my father, the king?'

The prince walked silently over to her and ran a hand contemptuously over the globes of her breasts. Sahria struggled vainly until the pain caused by the clawing of her shackles against her tender flesh became intense. 'I demand to know where my father is, you vermin!'

she screamed.

'You are in no position to demand anything, sweet princess. Your father has fled like a coward. I am king now, and you will do my bidding.'

'Never!' shouted Sahria, twisting her body awkwardly. The rings piercing her sex lips tugged fiercely at her tenderness and induced a copious flow from within her lust-wracked body, the juices seeping between her buttocks. The prince pinched her nipple hard, which forced her to cry out in pain.

'You will learn to obey me, princess,' he said calmly. He rolled the throbbing, erect nipple between his fingers before again digging the nails into the tortured flesh. 'Your days of domination are over. No longer will you be able to treat your lovers like animals, beating them into submission. Now *you* are the victim, and you will learn to love your acquiescence.'

Sahria lay back her head on the harsh wooden board. Her anger, whilst still powerful, was subsiding as the incongruous warmth between her legs gave testament to her rising state of arousal. 'Will you kill me?' she said, her voice unusually meek and trembling.

Sarne smiled almost kindly and ran his hand over the smooth flatness of her stomach before resting it on her wet pussy. He cupped the hot flesh with his palm, his skin feeling rough against her, and then he probed between the parted lips with searching fingers. He shook his head. 'No, that would be a terrible waste,' he replied, simply. His tongue slid across his upper lip as he watched her hips begin to move in suppliant response to his intimate caress. 'No,' he continued. 'There are many games I would have you play, and much that you must learn.'

'And if I refuse?'

Sarne squeezed her soft mound harshly, the sudden pressure causing her to wince. 'You will not refuse,' he said severely. 'You will learn to obey and, when I am satisfied that you have become the most compliant of creatures this prize will be yours.' He drew back his cloak and gripped his fierce erection proudly, once more presenting it to her like a trophy. She gazed in wonder at its hugeness. If anything, it seemed larger than she remembered it.

She began to shake involuntarily. The prince grinned. 'Ah, sweet child, you still yearn for it, don't you? You still dream of the day that this massive stalk will slide like a rigid serpent within your succulent sheath, do you not, my angel?'

He gripped her pussy cruelly, his fingernails clawing at her wet flesh. Sahria stared hungrily at his cock and pushed her mound against his palm, breathing heavily, her arousal complete. Apparently sensing her imminent release the prince pulled abruptly away from her and put his glistening fingers to his mouth. The princess glared at him, her anger rising once more.

Sarne breathed in deeply and then licked his fingertips slowly. 'Such a scent! Such a taste!'

Sahria decided to attempt a different approach. 'Enter me, prince,' she mewed softly. 'Fill me with that fine rod and let me draw the juices from you. You will not be sorry.'

Sarne continued to savour the taste on his fingertips with the occasional lap of his tongue. 'Your powers are legendary, princess,' he said, 'and I realise that I am denying myself many delights. But, until you are my slave completely there can be little pleasure in merely taking your body. Compliance without total capitulation is worthless.'

Sahria breathed heavily in exasperation. 'Am I to lie here, unsated and in pain for the rest of my life?' The princess felt a strange though unwelcome pleasure at the thought.

Sarne walked towards the open door. 'You will be freed in an hour, when you have had time to consider my words. You will be brought to the throne room, *my* throne room, and once there you will obey my every command.'

He made to walk out of the dungeon and then stopped, turning slowly to face her again. 'But beware, princess,' he continued in a quiet but menacing tone. 'Should you fail me you will know true pain.'

The door swung heavily on its rusty hinges and clanged to a close behind him. The rasp of iron bolts echoed against the damp stone walls and she was alone again in her misery. An eerie silence pervaded the atmosphere, save for the incessant dripping of water somewhere in the near darkness.

Sahria relaxed her body and closed her eyes, the ache between her legs subsiding slowly as she began to contemplate her predicament. The wetness beneath her bottom felt cold now, and she couldn't understand why she had become so incredibly aroused. Her years of holding a position of total domination had not prepared her for this and yet, oddly, she felt excited by the prospect of the unknown. What had he meant, should she fail him? His words spun around inside her head. What terrible delights awaited her in the throne room?

The hour was past all too quickly. The familiar sound of sliding bolts shattered the silence and the old door swung open. Two burly black slaves, the same two who had abused her so wickedly the night before walked into the room, one of them carrying a brightly flaming torch. Both were naked, there manhoods hanging heavily from their muscular bodies and their ebony skin aglow with a fresh sheen of sweat.

Sahria readied herself, certain that they were about to take her yet again. At least now she would be sated.

To her profound disappointment however, the slaves merely busied themselves with her shackles and roughly withdrew the thin chains from her pussy rings. They then untied the leather straps that had bound her limbs to tightly to her uncomfortable bed. One of the men, the larger of the two, took hold of the chains that were still fixed to her pierced nipples and yanked them hard, forcing her to rise painfully from the wooden board and stand before them. Her body ached and she found some difficulty in remaining fully erect. She leant back slightly until her bottom rested against the edge of the bench. The slave tugged the chain again sharply and grinned broadly when she cried out, more from shock than pain. Sahria glared at him defiantly but he simply returned her gaze, staring her fully in the face. That was something he would never have dared to do before.

Sahria looked down below his torso and saw that his cock was swiftly rising to a strong erection. He was enjoying this. Taking pleasure in her subjugation. She felt she should be angry, but instead sensed nothing but arousal. She yearned to grab the thick black stalk but thought better of it. The slaves were in control now.

The big man turned to the door and wrenched again at the chains joined to her aching nipples, causing her to follow him meekly into the brightly lit corridor. The other slave followed, pushing her unnecessarily in the back with a clenched fist.

Slowly they ascended the long steep stairway. Sahria's heart was pounding. More passageways, some unfamiliar to her, then more steps until, at last they entered the palatial magnificence of the throne room.

To her dismay, Sahria saw that the great hall was filled with people – peasants, nobles and slaves mixing together like old comrades. Some of them she knew, but many were complete strangers to her.

The babble of voices ceased moments after they walked into the room and all eyes turned towards her as she was made to walk towards the throne itself. Prince Sarne sat in her father's place, casually rubbing his immensely long penis and grinning like a fool. She hated him for his arrogance in perching so nonchalantly in the king's place. She despised his lack of respect.

Her eyes darted about, a dissonant mixture of fearful trembling and abject arousal building up within her naked body. Despite her sheer loathing for the man, for some reason she felt the need to bow her head as she approached the prince. She stared sullenly at the marble floor. Its surface felt cold against her bare feet and she shivered noticeably.

The prince stood up and drew his cloak across his nakedness. 'Kneel,' he commanded. Sahria stood her ground. 'I said kneel!' The fury in the prince's tone was clear. Sahria took a deep breath and then slowly slipped to her knees. She winced as she heard the sounds of laughter and derision emanating from the gathered throng. The large slave stood at her side, holding the chains tautly as though he was restraining a wild dog.

'You see before you your princess,' mocked Sarne loudly as he addressed the crowd. He walked around the form of his captive then stood behind her and pressed the sole of his boot hard against her bottom. She fell forward to lie flat on her belly. The chains held by the slave tightened as she fell and her nipples were stabbed with sudden pain. She squealed loudly, her cry echoing around the great room.

The prince moved around her again and then crouched in front of her. He raised her by the shoulders until she was able to resume the kneeling position, her back curved and her bottom displayed to many of the onlookers.

'This was your queen,' he laughed. 'Once so proud but now so servile.' He suddenly reached under his cloak and pulled out his cock, which was still firmly erect. He pressed the bulbous head to her mouth. 'Suck!' he demanded loudly.

A murmur spread though the crowd. Sahria pursed her lips and turned her head away. Sarne grabbed the chains from the slave's grasp and wrenched them harshly, making her yell with the pain. 'I said suck!'

he shouted.

Sahria turned her face towards the menacing stalk and slowly opened her mouth, the trace of a tear running down her cheek. Sarne pushed forward and the plum-sized head of his thick cock touched her pouting lips. She pulled away again and looked imploringly up at his face. Her features were now wet with the tears of shame and embarrassment.

'Please, my lord, not here,' she begged. 'Not here, in front of this crowd.'

'But yes, princess,' said Sarne, gripping her hair and pulling her face back towards his huge phallus. 'Before this crowd of peasants and beggars, of once noble lords and of servants. All are equal here, and all will see and savour this moment. Suck! Suck like you've never sucked before.'

Once more his spongy flesh was pressed against her. Sahria opened her mouth and moved her head forward, taking him between her wet lips. His thickness filled her mouth and caused her jaw to ache. She sensed the crowd drawing closer, hearing them chattering like excited children. She felt utterly ashamed, being prone and nakedly vulnerable before them, and yet the ache deep in her loins grew with each second as she held the prince's stalk within her mouth.

She suckled gently, feeling him throb against her tongue as it slid against his hardness. She swallowed, taking as much of him into her mouth as she could whilst gripping his bone-hard flesh with her pouting lips, and then reaching up to grasp the remainder of his length with both hands.

She began to rub him quickly, sucking hard and

occasionally taking him from her mouth and licking the end sensuously. She was now thoroughly engrossed in her task and loving every minute. For a moment the crowd of onlookers was forgotten as she savoured the taste of the biggest, hardest cock she had ever seen in her life.

'See, your princess surrenders to me and knows her master!' bellowed the prince. 'No longer is she your ruler. She is nothing more than your slave.'

Sahria was oblivious to his words. She held his cock erect with one hand and suckled his balls before running the tip of her tongue up the length of his shaft until she once more took the huge end into the warmth of her succulent mouth.

Without losing him from her heavenly grip she looked about her and saw the leering faces of the crowd as they pressed ever closer and craned their necks to enjoy this fine demonstration of her total humiliation. She closed her eyes to the sight and rubbed him harder, sucking him for all that she was worth.

Suddenly she felt him stiffen and heard him groan softly as his erection took on even more monstrous proportions within the wet envelope of her suckling mouth. Its thickness almost choked her. He groaned again, much louder this time and he gripped her head with both of his hands, allowing the chains to fall from his fingers to the floor. She felt his hard flesh throbbing against her lips and tongue as the warmth of his seed filled the back of her mouth and forced her to swallow quickly. Letting go of his cock with one of her hands but still sucking voraciously she grasped herself between the legs and clawed at her soaking sex flesh.

The crowd cheered wildly as though encouraging her to reach her own orgasm. Frantically she rubbed her aching bud until a sudden wave of ecstasy hit her, her cry of pleasure muffled by the slowly wilting monster still clasped within her tight mouth.

The prince pulled away from her and she allowed the thick, flaccid cock to slip from her mouth then she fell sobbing to the floor, her emotions confused and her entire body trembling. She sensed that Prince Sarne was standing over her, staring down at her submissive form and somehow knew that he was grinning inanely again. She closed her eyes and began to sob heavily, wrapping her arms around her head. The rhythm of her pounding heart matched the throbbing between her legs as the intensity of her release subsided. She had done well, she thought. The prince would be pleased with her.

She sensed him move and once more felt sharp pain in her breasts as the chains were pulled taut. Unwillingly, she rose to her feet with her head bowed, to ashamed to look into the faces of the leering throng. The prince reached forward and lifted her face with his fingertips. He held her gaze for a moment with an almost hypnotic stare. 'From this moment you are no longer a princess,' he said, strongly. 'Now you are Sahria, sex slave to the court of Prince Sarne!'

Sahria's look of shame changed to one of total hatred. 'You will never subjugate me, Sarne,' she hissed. 'I am nobody's slave!'

'We will see,' answered the prince, his grin broadening. He shoved her backwards and she fell onto her bottom with her legs splayed widely apart. A momentous cheer filled the room and the crowd applauded and danced in mock celebration. Sahria bowed her head again, her tears falling to the cold, uncaring marble floor.

Chapter Two

Prince Sarne leered contemptuously at the prone form of Princess Sahria. They were alone now, the crowd having been summarily dismissed by the prince following Sahria's humiliation. She crouched naked on the cold marble floor with her head bowed in shame.

'What think you now, princess?' The prince's tone was cruel and mocking while, at the same time making it clear that he was revelling in his brief victory. Sahria raised her head wearily and looked him full in the eye. Her hatred burned intentionally within her stony gaze.

'My lord?' she answered quietly.

'What think you, now that your people have witnessed your complete shame and subjugation? Your reputation has been dashed forever.'

She moved to a sitting position and drew her knees against her breasts, clutching her legs tightly as though attempting to conceal her nakedness from his lustful leer. She could feel the hardness of her nipples pressing against her cool skin, and their evident arousal annoyed her. 'You may have me in your power for the moment, Sarne, but that will not always be so. One day, not too far away, I will see to it that you regret your devilish deeds with all your heart.'

Prince Sarne reached down and touched her under the chin with his fingertips. She looked again into his eyes and, for a brief instant she sensed tenderness in his expression. 'We need not be enemies, princess,' he said, the gentleness in his tone sounding less than sincere.

'You defeated my father. You forced him to flee his country and desert his people.' Her throat was dry and she had to fight to get the words out without choking.

'Your father is a warrior. He fought bravely in battle. He may yet return, but you can be assured that I will be more than ready to meet any challenge he may throw down to me.'

'Why did you make war against my people?' Sahria managed to control her voice, speaking calmly and without emotion despite the fact that she detested this man for all he'd done to her. For some reason that was difficult to understand, she found the power that seemed to exude from his presence to be overtly stimulating. Sahria was unsure whether it was his hungry good looks, his deeply penetrating stare, or merely the mental image of his superb cock that caused her to tremble inside, but concluded that it was probably a mixture of all three. His dominant stance intrigued as well as excited her...

'Your country is rich and the land is fertile,' the prince continued. 'Why should you be surprised that your neighbours covet your wealth? It is well known that this very palace houses many priceless baubles looted from the farthest reaches of the world. And your women – they are well known for their beauty and their insatiable libidos. Why should I deny the men of my nation such delights?'

'And yourself,' muttered Sahria to herself.

'Above all, however,' continued Sarne, clearly not having heard her words, 'the fact is that your people were oppressed. I have come to free them from their yoke of submission.'

'By killing them?' Sahria pulled herself to her feet and glared angrily at the seated prince. The sarcasm in her tone seemed lost on him.

'There were few casualties, other than the trained soldiers whose lot it was to die for their king.' He regarded her through narrowed eyes. 'Princess Sahria,' he continued, 'you must learn to accept that your country is mine and that I am your ruler.'

Sahria placed her hands on her hips and stood squarely before him. She was no longer concerned about her nakedness, and in fact thrust her breasts forward in a defiant gesture. 'I will never bow before you, Sarne!' she exclaimed.

Sarne leered at her sumptuous flesh and smiled cruelly. 'You bowed enough when I fed your sweet mouth with my thick stalk,' he sneered.

'I had little choice, shackled as I was to your slave. You are a coward, Sarne.'

The prince leapt angrily from his seat and towered above her. He gripped her arms tightly and she struggled vainly as his fingernails dug into her soft flesh. 'You are the coward, princess,' he roared. 'For years you have tormented your subjects to satisfy your carnal needs. Now you will learn for yourself the true pleasures of pain and subjugation!'

He pushed her away roughly and she fell heavily to the floor, with her legs splayed apart. Sarne looked unashamedly at her exposed sex. Sahria made no attempt to cover herself, defiantly offering her body to his eager gaze. 'You have a succulent pussy,' he said, his voice softer in tone. 'I wonder how many hard pricks it has accommodated over the years.'

Sahria said nothing in response but found, to her profound irritation, that her juices were beginning to flow again and were already trickling between her buttocks. She closed her legs and clutched her knees against herself once more. Sarne knelt in front of her and forced her thighs apart. 'No, don't hide your treasures, princess,' he said, as he looked down at her shivering nakedness. He ran the tip of his tongue across the surface of his upper lip as he leered at her. 'See how it glistens, reflecting the sunlight,' he breathed, his voice barely audible, even to her.

Sensing a kind of victory, Sahria rested her hands on the floor behind her and leant back, thrusting her breasts upward and spreading her legs as wide as was possible. She sensed her sex lips part to offer him the tantalising view of her inner flesh. 'Why don't you fuck me, Prince Sarne of Persia?' she taunted. 'Why don't you get it over with?'

There was a long pause as the prince gazed at the open lips of her cunt. He reached forward and tugged lightly at one of the rings that pierced her tender sex flesh. 'I will fuck you when I am ready,' he said quietly, 'but first you must learn.'

'Learn what?' Sahria pushed his hand away and struggled to her feet. She waited for a moment, but there was no response. Sarne merely looked at her, his expression betraying little emotion. She turned her back on him angrily and strode across the hall.

'Come back here!' The prince's voice boomed out and echoed around the room. Sahria turned to face him and glared.

'Just who do you think you're talking to?' she growled. 'I am not one of your slaves.'

Sarne walked quickly over to her and grabbed her by the arm. She tried to pull away but his grip was too fierce. 'There are no slaves here,' he hissed, 'not any more. All men are free.'

Sahria laughed in his face. 'You are a fool. A rich man must have his slaves. How else is he to live?'

The prince answered by grasping her hair and roughly pressing his mouth to hers. She felt him probing his tongue between her lips and clenched her teeth tightly to deny him entry. He gripped her bottom with his free hand and pressed his crotch against her. She could feel the hardness of his thick erection against her stomach. She allowed her mouth to relax and his tongue slid against her own. For a brief moment she tried to imagine what it would feel like to have that same tongue slithering in and out of her hot pussy in preparation for even greater joys to come. Suddenly, she regained her composure and bit him firmly on the lower lip. He yelped and pushed her away with such a force that she once again fell to the hard, marble floor.

'You evil vixen,' he moaned as he grasped his bleeding mouth. 'You'll pay dearly for such gross impertinence.' He clapped his hands loudly. Immediately, three guards appeared as if from nowhere. 'Take this to the black chamber,' he ordered, as he indicated Sahria's naked form. The guards looked at one another and grinned, then roughly helped her to her feet. She was furious at their treatment of her but was trembling visibly. Sahria knew the secrets of the black chamber well. She had enjoyed many diversions there in the past, watching as the men were shackled and beaten, purely for her own lascivious delight. Now it appeared it was to be she who was the victim.

Two of the guards gripped her wrists while the third stood behind her and pressed his spear against her naked back. She looked over her shoulder and glared with utter contempt at the armed man.

'Just where do you think I'm going, dressed in nothing but my own sweat?' she hissed. 'Put the weapon down, you fool. I am a princess. I will walk on my own.' She shook her arms free of the other guards and marched purposefully towards the door.

'You will learn much this night,' called the prince from behind her, his voice still shaking with fury. 'You will discover the pleasures of pain, and you will come to me begging for more!'

Sahria ignored him, contemptuously tossing back her hair as she continued to walk swiftly from the hall, closely followed by the guards.

Once they were out of the prince's sight one of the soldiers ran a hand over the sumptuous curves of her bottom. She grabbed hold of his wrist and flung it away from her. 'Touch me again, you animal,' she spat, 'and you will pay with your life!'

The guards laughed in roars of united derision. The first reached out his hand and fondled her buttocks roughly, then wormed a finger against her anus. The second guard held his spear against her throat and stared into her eyes menacingly, while the third soldier cupped her pussy.

'She is soaked!' he exclaimed with a grin. 'She is already prepared for us, my friends.'

Sahria tried to push his hand away, but in vain. He slipped all four fingers deep inside her and she groaned, not with pain but with pleasure.

'See, this is what she wants,' the guard continued. 'Let us have some sport with her.'

Regardless of the fact that she was trembling with sheer anger at their impertinence, Sahria felt an overwhelming desire to give herself to these rough-handed men. The events in the great hall had fired both her imagination and her lust.

The soldier behind her had managed to force his finger fully inside her bottom and was moving it rhythmically in and out, like a tiny, hard penis. Her breathing became laboured and she sensed her juices flowing. Despite her previous years engaged in many and varied libidinous pursuits, she had never been touched in such a base way before. Nobody would have dared.

'I said take her to the black chamber!' The voice was that of Prince Sarne, who was suddenly standing behind them. He was clearly furious. The two men immediately withdrew their hands from Sahria's nether regions and pushed her forward before the prince could wreak his vengeance on them. They rounded a corner quickly in the passageway and then slowed their steps.

'I thought we were done for then,' said one of them as he breathed hard. He glanced fearfully over his shoulder, but the prince had not followed them.

'It could have been our heads,' babbled another.

'Why do you serve such a vicious master?' queried Sahria, anxious to win these slow-witted numbskulls in some small way.

'He is strong but he is fair,' replied the spear-carrying guard. 'In our country he freed all the slaves and gave work to the beggars. He intends to do the same in your own land, now that he has rid the country of the tyrant Al Fahoud.'

'Take care when you speak of my father—' Sahria began.

'He is an evil man, and you know it. The people lived in constant dread, never knowing if each day was to be their last.' The soldier stroked one of her breasts, then cupped the mound of flesh. Sahria remained nonchalant, as though he was gripping her wrist. His bony, rough-skinned fingers squeezed her breast and she bit her lip, determined not to show her pain. 'Now the people are free, to do as they please,' he added.

'And there are many other delights, as you will soon learn,' said the soldier who had previously slipped his finger inside her bottom.

'What do you mean, other delights?' Sahria asked the question, but feared that she already knew the answer.

'You will see... you will see.'

They were nearing the door to the black chamber. Sahria began to feel a nervous fluttering in the pit of her stomach. She had never been slapped, let alone restrained and lashed as her own victims had been. Was she to be shackled to one of the many frames in the room and beaten? Or was there much worse in store for her?

The spear was rapped against the door four times. Presently she heard the drawing of bolts and the heavy wooden barrier was opened. A small but immensely muscular man stood before her, wearing nothing but a tattered and grimy loincloth. His face bore an expression of utter evil as he leered at her through tiny, pig-narrow eyes.

'Lord Rapite,' one of the guards said in a formal tone of voice. 'Prince Sarne has ordered you to play host to the Princess Sahria.'

The small man walked slowly around her, eyeing her up as if he was considering the purchase of a slave in the market. She shuddered. He reached up and weighed one of her breasts in his gnarled hand. His skin felt as rough as old wood. He pinched her nipple and then tugged sharply at the ring that pierced the erect bud. Sahria winced with pain, but did not cry out.

'A fine specimen,' he growled. 'I shall enjoy taming this one.'

'She has a pussy that runs like a river,' said one of the guards. The small man took this as an invitation and cupped her wet mound with his free hand. He gripped the soft flesh tightly and slipped a couple of fingers inside her. Sahria stiffened her thigh muscles, but was unable to halt the unwelcome intrusion.

'Indeed she has,' he leered. He stepped back and sniffed his wet fingertips, then bowed mockingly. 'Quite delicious,' he said with a grin. He made a gesture with his arm to indicate that she should pass

42

by him. 'Enter, my dear princess, enter my chamber of pleasure. When you again see the light of day you will be a changed woman.'

Sahria walked meekly into the darkened room. Rapite followed her and closed the old door noisily, barring it immediately with the many bolts. Sahria looked around the grim room slowly. Two flickering torches illuminated numerous racks and frames, as well as a myriad of other items of restraint, casting eerie shadows about the place. The walls were festooned with whips, flails and canes.

The chamber was little changed from the last time she had visited it, but this time it would be she who was shackled. It would be she who would feel the pain of the tawse or the rod, the rough grip of the iron cuffs and, above all, the kiss of the lash.

Rapite moved over to one of the frames. To Sahria's eyes it resembled one of the easels used by the court artists, but was much larger. Four leather straps were fixed to the gnarled wood by heavy iron rings, two at the top and two close to the base. The small man clambered onto an upturned box and began to unbuckle one of the higher straps. 'Come here, my dear,' he sneered. His intentions were clear and, in earlier times Sahria would have refused, but for some reason that was incomprehensible to her she now felt compelled to obey, as though drawn to a nameless fate.

She walked slowly forward. Rapite took hold of her arm roughly and raised it until he was able to secure her wrist within the grip of the leather bond. He drew the strap tightly and secured it within an iron buckle, then jumped down from his perch and turned her to face the frame. He scuttled below her like the rat that he resembled, deftly anchoring her legs by the ankles to the two supports, and ensuring that her feet were spread widely apart and her body was facing the frame in a pose of abject submission. Finally, he clambered onto another box and completed his task by securing the remaining leather strap around her other wrist and pulling it tight. This time it hurt – it hurt a lot, but somehow the pain warmed her.

Rapite jumped down once more and stood behind her as if to survey the quality of his work. Throughout his activities Sahria remained impassive. She knew there was little chance of escape, but above all she found her curiosity was fired. She'd had similar feelings in the past, notably during the many occasions when she'd witnessed the sensuous flogging of her many conquests. She had often wondered what it would be like to be shackled, naked and helpless, completely at the mercy of her tormentor. Her rank at court had meant that she could never allow herself to be placed in such a vulnerable position, of course. Now things were very much different and, incongruously she realised that her feelings were more tinged with sexual excitement than with fear.

There was a long pause, the silence broken only by her captor's heavy breathing. She knew he was looking closely at her and examining every curve of her body. She felt him touch her bottom with his fingertips, and shivered. He knelt behind her and parted her buttocks with his thumbs. She could feel his hot breath against her anus and sex lips. He kissed her lightly on her tiny sphincter, then ran his tongue slowly from her anus upwards to the small of her back. For a few seconds she felt angry at his affront. How dare this pig of a man lick the royal bottom? Despite her annoyance, however, she sensed her inner thighs becoming saturated with her own juices.

'Such a fine arse,' the evil man muttered, as though to some unseen audience. 'It would seem a shame to mark such perfect globes.'

'Then why mark them?' Sahria said slowly. 'Why not continue to enjoy them as you have been doing, with your hands and your tongue?' Shackled as she was, she found the idea quite entertaining, although the very thought of allowing the repulsive man to do anything more intimate than she had just suggested was quite out of the question.

'Silence, vixen,' he commanded, his tone reminding her that she had little choice in the matter. He slapped her bottom hard with the palm of his hand. 'In the black chamber you may not speak without my permission.'

Sahria gritted her teeth, determined not to show him that the slap had stung her bottom quite severely. For a few moments he seemed to take her at her word and fondled her buttocks with all the finesse and desire of an expert lover. Sahria allowed herself to relax a little, despite her limbs being stretched painfully by her position against the frame. She breathed deeply as his fingers explored the outer lips of her pussy. She yearned for him to touch her aching clitoris and to give her the release she craved, but he seemed to be purposely avoiding contact with the hard little bud.

He moved away, and she heard him picking

something up in the darkness behind her. She turned her head as best she could to see he was holding a vicious, long-handled whip that boasted at least a dozen strands of thin leather, splaying from the tightly bound end. She turned her face away from him and braced herself for the inevitable thrashing. She began to tremble as she remembered the way the lash had cut into the sinewy flesh of her male victims, and considered with some justification that her delicate skin would be torn to shreds.

She felt him caress her back with the cool lengths of leather. He moved the lashes up and down her spine as if taunting her with their gentle touch. Her shoulders were beginning to ache and she could feel the blood in her wrists thumping as it forced its way through the tight restraints. Suddenly, there was a loud crack as the whip was brought down on a table. Sahria gasped and jumped visibly. Rapite laughed, a cruel cackle.

'Are you afraid, dear princess? Speak!'

'No, I am not afraid,' she lied.

He stood at her side and leered up at her face. 'Then you should be, princess,' he snarled, 'for you know full well that the lash will cut into your tender skin, and that the pain will be excruciating.'

'Do as you wish, Rapite. You cannot break my will.' Sahria was trembling quite markedly, much to her disappointment. She had not wished to show any terror to this dreadful man. He could lash her for all he was worth and beat her into unconsciousness for all she cared, but she was determined not to reveal any weakness.

There was another long pause. Sahria waited for the

first stroke of the foul weapon against her soft skin. Her nipples felt erect against the hard wood of the frame. Her pussy throbbed involuntarily and she began to slowly realise that she *wanted* the pain. She needed him to lash her with such force that the searing strips of leather would tear her flesh, just as he had promised.

'Why do you wait, Rapite?' she murmured. 'Why not be done with it?'

'I told you not to speak unless I gave you permission,' he said angrily, his voice becoming louder and more menacing with each word. 'Now you will be severely punished!'

Sahria heard him drop the whip onto the table. She turned her head again and saw him take up a thin strip of bamboo. He moved back to stand at her side and tickled her bottom with the end of the cane. 'You are not ready for the whip yet. You need to learn the many pleasures of pain before you can be subjected to the ultimate agony and delight. This will be merely a taster of the many joys to come.'

She saw him raise his muscular arm above his head and turned her face away to stare at the wall. She stiffened her buttocks. The cane swished through the air, but there was no contact with her body. Rapite did the same again, and then repeated it a third time, teasing her mercilessly. Sahria cursed him under her breath. The heat between her legs was becoming almost unbearable.

The sudden swish of the cane startled her and the searing agony she felt across her buttocks caused her to cry out. She clawed at the wood of the frame with her fingernails and gritted her teeth. The pain had been

47

far more intense than she'd ever imagined it could be, and now she wasn't so sure how much she would be able to take. The air swished again and she was cut a second time. It became painfully apparent to her that Rapite was a master at his craft. The cane had bitten into her flesh in exactly the same place as the first time it scored her plump flesh.

The third stroke was the worst. It cut her at the tops of her thighs, just under the delicate swell of her bottom. She shrieked with the pain, and was immediately furious with herself for having done so. She felt she was showing herself up as nothing more than a pathetic woman, and vowed never to cry out again.

At least ten more cuts followed. Sahria lost the will to count them. Her bottom was almost numb, and the pain had become far less severe. Rapite eventually started to grunt with exhaustion, clearly through putting every effort into his labours. The last couple of strokes barely stung her.

At last, Rapite threw the cane onto the table and sat on the box next to her, panting heavily. Sahria felt a tear trickling from her eye and turned her face away from him, lest he sense her vulnerability. She managed to wipe the tear from her cheek onto her upper arm, then looked back at the sweating man. She held his gaze with a cold stare.

'You took it well, princess,' he wheezed. 'I have seen many a strong man beg for mercy after the first cut.'

Sahria chose to ignore his barbed compliment. The feeling was returning to her tortured buttocks, and the pain seemed to be increasing rather than decreasing as her nerve-endings became once more fired with sensation. Strangely, however, the more her bottom ached, the more her sexual arousal increased. She had even come close to orgasm during the beating, but it had not been enough. She realised now why so many of the men she had thrashed in the past had fallen from their shackles with raging erections. She had thought it most peculiar; thinking it to be perhaps an odd physical reaction to intense pain, and it had amused her. Now she understood.

After a few more minutes Rapite rose to his feet and moved behind her. Sahria felt him stroke her stinging bottom with his callused hands, and once more sensed the fluids of her arousal slipping from her pouting sex lips to dampen her inner thighs.

'You are well marked,' he said proudly. 'The prince will be most pleased.'

'May I speak, my lord?' she asked weakly.

'You may.'

Sahria took a deep breath. 'Is this my lot, to remain shackled here for the rest of my life?'

Rapite laughed as he continued to fondle her aching buttocks. 'No, dear princess, this is merely a beginning. Prince Sarne is most inventive when it comes to the pleasures of humiliation. I am certain that he has many far more bizarre delights in store for you.'

'And if I do not submit?'

'You will be sent to me for punishment and, believe me, it will not always be so pleasurable.'

'Do you take pleasure in your work?' she asked. 'You seem so exhausted after punishing me.'

'There are no greater delights in life than the sight of a plump bottom quivering under the cane, and the sounds of anguished screams as the scourge cuts into unbroken flesh.'

Sahria had to admit to herself that the evil torturer spoke the truth. 'What if I were to offer to assist the prince?' she said. 'Do you think he would allow it?'

'The prince is always keen to learn of new diversions, and your reputation goes before you, princess. Firstly, however, he must be convinced that your submission to him is complete.' As he spoke he began to worm a finger inside her tight little anus.

'Must you abuse me so?' she implored.

'Silence!' he roared. 'You are in no position to deny me anything!'

'Yes, my lord,' she sighed.

'In fact, I think I may fuck you,' her tormentor said as he slipped his finger from within its tight sheath.

'Not there,' she said firmly. 'I would not even allow a prince to enter that forbidden place.'

Rapite laughed. 'As I said, you are in no position to refuse me anything.'

Sahria looked round at him and caught his eye with a steely glare. 'That may be true while you have me shackled here like a slave, but if you dare do that to me then I swear one day I will kill you.'

The grin disappeared from Rapite's face. Sahria knew it would have been clear from her stony expression that she had meant every word. There was a long and uncomfortable silence.

Presently he shrugged. 'It is not my desire to impale you in such a way,' he said, his voice sounding like that of a small child who had been denied a childish pleasure. 'But be warned, the prince has a penchant for the pleasures of Sodom, and he will not be so readily denied.'

'I will deal with that when necessary,' replied Sahria. Her mind was immediately filled with pictures of Prince Sarne thrusting his huge weapon into her virginal orifice. She breathed deeply, convinced that such a thing would not be possible.

'And now I will take my payment,' breathed Rapite. Sahria glanced down and saw his grubby loincloth fall to the floor. She turned her head in order to see his nakedness, but he moved quickly behind her and gripped her hips tightly with both hands. She could feel the swollen end of his erection touching her bottom. The difference in their heights and the way her legs were spread wide apart made the position ideal for penetration.

'I warn you…' she cautioned.

'Fear not, dear princess. It is your other, soft and soaked entrance that I most desire.'

Sahria was in neither the position nor the mood to refuse him. He was ugly, small in stature and reeked of the dungeon, but she needed sex badly, and she needed it now.

She felt him move his penis against her. He rolled the plum-shaped end around her outer lips without entering her. He was teasing her again, as he had with the cane. She wanted to cry out to him and beg him to ram his stiffness into her aching sheath, but she knew he would merely torment her all the more if she uttered a sound. She bent her back, straining her tortured wrists and ankles against the leather restraints and sharp buckles in order to force her bottom out in a provocative pose. But his response was to move away from her. Sahria cursed him again under her breath.

She sensed the touch of his thumbs once more parting the cheeks of her bottom, and then felt the heavenly wetness of his tongue as it circled around the open lips of her sex. She stiffened her legs in an effort to force her orgasm, but he seemed to perceive her desire and moved the tip of his tongue from her pussy, and instead lapped hungrily around the sumptuous globes of her bottom. Normally she would have enjoyed the sensation, but not this time. She desperately needed to be impaled and to feel a stiff cock deep within her loins.

He moved from her, and it seemed he was just standing motionless, looking at her. She turned her head. She could see his full nakedness now, and the sight was not altogether unpleasant. His cock, although not overly long, was extremely thick. It jutted firmly upwards, the veins standing proud in bold relief. He was clearly highly aroused, and yet was somehow managing to hold himself back from her proffered delights. Sahria wondered at the man's self-control. She also pondered as to whether he would be able to maintain this control when he finally entered her soaking honeypot, or if he would fill her with his cream the moment his fat cock became enveloped by her succulent flesh. She was fully aware that she desperately needed a good long fuck to make up for the teasing and the torment she had endured.

He moved behind her again and she turned once

more to face the wall. Surely he would take her now? No man had ever before been so reticent to ram his weapon into her. His swollen knob touched her sex lips again and he recommenced his agonisingly delightful circular movements, opening her without entering her sweet chalice. She began to tremble violently.

'Ah, princess,' he breathed malevolently, 'you are hot for it, are you not?'

'Yes, my lord,' she panted in reply. 'I yearn for you to fill me with your wondrous stalk.'

He sniggered cruelly and began to slide the wet end of his tool up and down along the cleft of her bottom. Sahria considered for a brief instant that she would even let him take her *there*, in that forbidden place, so badly did she need to feel him inside her body. But no, that was not right; she could not allow such a thing. Whatever they said, she was still a princess.

He pressed the head of his cock against her tight virgin sphincter, and she tensed in order to stop him violating her there. But she heard him chuckle. It was as he had insisted; in her restrained position she would have no choice. He could do to her whatever he pleased. If he wanted to fuck her in the bottom he could. She braced herself in readiness for the pain, but he moved suddenly and forced his full length deep into her welcoming cunt with one harsh jab. She cried out, more from shock than relief. He held himself still. She could feel him stretching her tight flesh, sensed him throb within her, and prayed shamefully that he hadn't come. She needed more – much more.

He gripped her stinging buttocks and dug his

fingernails into her soft globes, causing her to wince with the pain. Steadily, he began to move in and out of her. At last she was getting the fuck she so desperately craved.

The thickness of his rod caused her some discomfort at first, and she began to wonder if she would ever be able to accommodate Prince Sarne's mighty weapon. Rapite matched the prince for thickness, but was probably less than half his length.

Such thoughts were driven from her mind, however, as her inner muscles became accustomed to the stiff intrusion and he moved steadily in and out of her. She moaned softly and relaxed. Normally she would have responded to her lover's movements with wild thrusts of her own, but such behaviour was impossible, tethered as she was to the unyielding frame.

He started to plunge in and out of her with urgent purpose. Sahria matched the rhythm of his thrusts with her laboured breathing, occasionally moaning loudly with the sheer delight of the moment. The searing heat between her legs was building fast. Her release was imminent. 'Yes... yes... *harder*!' she cried involuntarily. She was close, very close. 'Yes... yes...' she cried again. 'I'm coming, I'm *coming*...'

Rapite suddenly withdrew from her and laughed as she whimpered. Her moment had been cruelly snatched from her. 'Please,' she sobbed, '*please*...'

'Ah no, sweet princess,' he sneered, 'you seem to forget that you are here for punishment.'

Sahria began to sob uncontrollably and her tears streamed down her soft cheeks. Her sex was on fire. She stiffened the muscles of her inner thighs in a desperate attempt to take herself over the edge, but it was too late. The urgency had passed. Suddenly she hated the man with venom that was unknown, even to her.

Rapite stroked her bottom with an incongruous tenderness. She relaxed again. His touch, although insufficient for her rapacious needs, was at least soothing. His fingers felt rough and the nails snagged her skin, but the caress seemed strangely delicate. She stopped sobbing, took a deep breath, and glanced over her shoulder. He was staring at her bottom with the expression of a man possessed. His stalk was as erect as before and glistened in the flickering torchlight. She turned her face away again, sadly. How could a man taunt her so? How could he taunt *himself* so?

Suddenly, and without warning, her bottom was once more seared with pain as he slapped her forcefully with the palm of a hand. Sahria yelped, and the sound of her cry echoed around the chamber. Another slap followed quickly, then another and another. Each one was delivered with such power that her breath was knocked from her body. The ache for release was rapidly building between her legs again. More slaps; five, ten, fifteen. His assault was unrelenting. He seemed to be possessed by some manic force as he rained blow after sweet blow against her quivering backside. Her pussy throbbed heavily and her juices flowed. The sounds of flesh striking stinging flesh reverberated against the damp stone walls of her prison.

The heat within her loins rose sharply and she knew she was beyond the point of no return. Her sex lips felt as though unseen fingers were tugging them apart, and her tiny bud seemed to be on fire. With a stabbing thrust of sheer pleasurable release she came at last. It was probably the most intense orgasm she had ever experienced, even more violent than the one she'd enjoyed whilst cruelly shackled in the dungeon that morning. She filled her lungs with the acrid air and then screamed as a thousand needles seemed to jab into her most intimate parts, over and over again.

Rapite slapped her six more times as she shuddered and climaxed again and again, but she was oblivious to the pain in her bottom. Every feeling, every sensation emanated from between her legs.

Slowly, she relaxed. Her breathing was heavy and her pussy was throbbing wildly. She peered wearily over her shoulder. Rapite was standing slightly to one side of her, masturbating openly. She watched as he massaged his thick stalk, until he grimaced and his cream jetted from the eye of the monster to streak across her glowing buttocks. His orgasm seemed endless. More and more of his juices gushed from him to soak her hot bottom, and she could feel the warmth of his release against the heat of her tortured skin.

When he was done he smoothed the juices over her bottom and massaged the cream into her soft flesh. A finger once more strayed into the tightness of her virgin anus, lubricated by a combination of their juices, and Sahria began to wonder if, one day, she might allow a lover to penetrate her in that most intimate place.

And then, once more she realised that she would probably have no choice in the matter.

Chapter Three

Sahria hung motionless in the silent darkness of her prison, her limbs aching and the tortured skin of her bottom feeling as though it was on fire. How long she had been there she couldn't guess. Time had ceased to have any meaning.

Rapite had extinguished the two torches and left her alone without a word. She seethed with hatred for the man. How dare he beat her? How dare he penetrate her body with his fat, ugly stalk? Once again, Sahria vowed revenge on him and on Prince Sarne. She silently swore to herself that one day they would bitterly regret their impudence!

She tugged weakly at one of the leather straps binding her wrists. The result of her action was a sharp stab of pain as the iron buckle bit into her flesh. She wondered fearfully how long she would be left to dangle like a piece of meat, naked and totally helpless. Perhaps it would be forever.

She shivered with the cold, and she was hungry.

Inextricably her thoughts turned full circle and she pictured herself lying prone on the cold stone floor as a dozen faceless men stood around her, openly masturbating until they sated themselves over her naked body. She imagined their pricks to be huge, jutting ghost-like within eerie clouds of translucent mist.

She began to sob quietly as her anger built once more within her cold body. How could she, a royal princess, find herself in such a vulnerable position? What was to become of her? Would she be left to die? Sahria felt utterly hopeless and wretched.

Her bottom began to sting again and her thoughts returned to the beating she had recently endured. The cane had cut deep, seeming in her imagination to tear the very flesh from her body. The sweat of terror had trickled down the backs of her thighs, but after the shock of the first three or four strokes the pain had become strangely pleasurable. The memory of her orgasm ripping through her loins like fire made her realise that she was beginning to crave for more.

She thought of the whip with which Rapite had initially teased her. She imagined the vicious strips of leather lashing her stiffened buttocks. Just the thought of it made her juices flow as her sex lips opened as if in readiness for some unseen lover. She wondered, more in hope than expectation, whether Rapite would return soon and this time take up the whip. She longed to hear the sounds of the door being unbolted and yearned to sense his squat form moving menacingly towards her as she hung helplessly at his mercy.

She tried to understand why she felt this way, although she knew in her heart that she quite simply craved the kiss of the lash. Thoughts of a queue of strong men waiting in line to thrash her filled her hungry imagination. She felt she could see their naked, oiled bodies and their rippling muscles. She imagined their faces covered with sweat as they whipped her mercilessly, and pictured their erections waving rhythmically as they laboured.

Her pussy ached for release and she clenched her inner thigh muscles to heighten the sensation. She tugged at the leather straps around her wrists and took pleasure in their unyielding restraint. They could do anything they wished to her. They could lash her, they could cut her with the cane, and they could slap her buttocks with their rough hands. When they tired of this, they could ram their stiff pricks into her soaked cunt. She would take them all, as many as wished to use and abuse her. Perhaps they would take her final virginity and fuck her bottom. The more she considered this ultimate penetration the more she found she quite liked the idea.

The queue would be endless. She would spend the rest of her life tied and trussed to be fucked and beaten. She began to shake with lust. Her clitoris ached to be touched by a finger, a tongue, or anything. She had never experienced such lascivious desires before. The feelings were overpowering. Damn Rapite, she thought, why didn't he return to the black chamber and at least cane her again?

She was desperate to come. She thought once more about the line of naked men, each carrying whips or vicious flails. She sensed that she could actually feel the pain as they lashed her poor bottom. Suddenly it was too much for her. A searing sensation of pure joy tore through her loins like a bolt of lightning as her orgasm took control of her very soul. She cried out involuntarily, the sound echoing around the grim stone walls of her prison. She shook violently as wave after wave of delicious sensations ripped through her body.

There was a loud crack and one of the leather straps binding her wrists snapped. Immediately she clutched her pussy with her freed hand and dug all four fingers into her wet flesh. She eased her thumb inside and curled her fingers to form a fist within her luscious pulsating grip. She plunged her hand in and out of her silken honeypot as a second wave of orgasmic joy hit her. She cried out again, then bit her lower lip painfully in order to stifle the sounds of her pleasure. She tried to imagine two, or even three men thrusting their massive pricks into her at the same time while others continued to lash her bottom in perfect unison. Her mind reeled as the pain of perfect release overtook her, screaming uncontrollably as the final joyous sensation turned her loins to fire. Her juices burned as they slipped from her and the hard bud of her clitoris felt as if it would burst.

At last, the feelings subsided and she eased her hand away. She gasped for breath, taking in the foul air gratefully. She put the tips of her fingers to her mouth and tasted the sweet nectar of her release. Prince Sarne had spoken the truth; she *had* become a slave to the lash. She knew that whatever happened, whatever they had in store for her, it would only serve to heighten her delight.

It was some time before Sahria became relaxed enough to use her free hand to unfasten the remaining three straps that bound her to the frame. At last she was free, at least of the painful restraint. She moved cautiously in the darkness until she found what felt like a small cot in a corner of the dungeon. She sat down and rubbed her tender joints. As the blood began to once more course through her veins the pain returned to her wrists and ankles. She lay back on the cot, drew the single rough sheet over her exhausted body, closed her eyes, and drifted into a deep sleep.

Sahria awoke with a start. She had been dreaming; a meandering vision which had suddenly turned into a nightmare of startling reality. She opened her eyes and attempted to make sense of the strange shapes in the darkness of the room. Suddenly she realised that the nightmare had been true. She was a prisoner in her own dungeon, held at the mercy of the evil Prince Sarne and his foul cohorts.

She made to sit up. The sudden ache in her bottom brought back vivid memories of her recent punishment, and she stood and stroked her buttocks carefully. Her fingertips traced the numerous welts left by the stinging rod, but she smiled to herself; it had been good.

She sat down again on the cot with her hands clasped between her thighs like a small child. There was nothing she could do. She had to wait – wait until Rapite returned. He would surely thrash her when he saw that she had managed to release herself from the frame. She pondered as to whether she should shackle herself again in the hope that he wouldn't notice one of the straps was broken, but thought better of it. What was the point? He would discover her deceit soon enough, and it would be all the worse for her.

Sahria lay back on the cot and drew the sheet over her nakedness once more. She closed her eyes and tried to imagine what forms the torture and humiliation

61

that awaited her might take.

Suddenly, she remembered Calema. How could she have been so selfish, so stupid? While she had been enjoying her pain at the hands of Rapite she hadn't given a moment's thought to her beautiful friend's whereabouts. Had she been harmed? Was she even alive?

She pictured Calema's lovely face, with its incongruously virginal expression and her innocent eyes that made men fall hopelessly in love with her at first sight. Little did they know her true insatiable appetite for pleasures of the flesh. When they learned the truth, of course they would take her lithe young body and enjoy her waif-like curves and apple-firm breasts. Many would think they were the first, and Calema did little to dissuade them. Sometimes they were, Sahria mused, at least that day.

She smiled as she remembered one particular time when Calema had pleasured eight men simultaneously. She could still picture the sight of her beautiful friend lying across the supine form of one man so that his cock slipped effortlessly inside her soaking pussy, while a second pushed his erection into her sweet and inviting bottom. Two more of the athletic hunks managed to push their raging stalks into her mouth, and Sahria could still visualise Calema's pouting lips stretched around their hard flesh. Reaching out with her hands, Calema had then grasped the pricks of two more willing victims and masturbated them expertly whilst rubbing the soles of her feet against yet two more!

How the court enjoyed her delicious demonstration.

And how desirable Calema had looked when they had sated themselves. Sahria could still see her, lying on the couch with her entire body, face and hair streaked with the cream of eight men's lust. Sahria saw Calema's happy face as if it were yesterday, a trickle of sperm slipping from the girl's cute lips, and her bright eyes sparkling with joy.

Sahria had to find her – and quickly.

Her thoughts were interrupted by the sounds of the bolts being drawn on the other side of the door. She jumped from the bed and stood proudly, her back arched and her breasts jutting firmly, ready to face her tormentor. A shaft of light broke through the oppressive darkness. Then suddenly, a small figure was pushed unceremoniously into the room and the door was slammed shut. The walls echoed to the sounds of the bolts being secured once more. The silence returned with the darkness, broken only by the quiet sobbing of the prone form on the cold stone floor.

Sahria's heart leapt. 'Calema?' she said excitedly, 'Calema, is that you?'

'Sahria? Oh, my dear sweet sister, I thought you were dead!' Calema's voice sang in the darkness and echoed Sahria's delight. Her eyes were better used to the blackness and she managed to clutch her friend's arm and help her to her feet. The two girls hugged each other tightly and let the tears flow.

'Oh, Calema,' sobbed Sahria, 'I thought it could be you who was lost. What have they done to you?'

'It is so strange, sister. There was pain, but there was also so much pleasure. I could never have imagined having so much joy.'

Sahria helped her to sit on the cot and wrapped the sheet around the girl's shoulders, and then sat next to her. 'Tell me what happened,' she said.

'Well, I was walking in the forest with two handsome Nubian slaves,' Calema began. 'You may remember that my father hates me to consort with the Nubians, but you will also know how much I enjoy the sight of their ebony flesh. These two were particularly fine specimens, and very compliant.' Despite their predicament, she couldn't suppress an impish grin at the thought of them. 'I had just beaten them soundly with rough branches which they obediently cut from a spruce, and was just about to impale myself on one of their delicious cocks when we were interrupted by a messenger.'

'You know that my father, the king, has fled the country?' said Sahria quietly.

Calema nodded. 'Yes,' she said softly, 'but I was told that he fought bravely. My own parents have vanished also, and I pray they have not been harmed.'

'The king would never allow them to suffer,' said Sahria carefully. 'Your father is his best friend. They will be safe.' Her words seemed to soothe Calema's grief in the same way that the knowledge of the king's bravado in battle helped Sahria.

'Carry on with your story,' she whispered.

'The messenger told me there had been a great battle, and that the kingdom was lost. I couldn't believe it. It had all happened so quickly.' Calema began to cry, and Sahria touched her face lightly.

'I, too, knew nothing until I awoke to find myself in

chains,' she said.

'Chains?' queried Calema.

Sahria detected a glint of excitement in her eyes. 'I'll tell you my story later. Go on.'

'I returned to the palace and was immediately arrested by the guards. There were five of them, five muscular men. I was at their mercy. I knew two of them, having seen them about the palace, but the other three were strangers to me. I was taken to their guardhouse. At first I thought they were merely going to imprison me, but once the door was closed it wasn't long before I realised they had other intentions.

'I was thrown roughly across the room and fell against a tattered old couch. One of the men picked up some rope and for a moment simply stood there, leering at me. I demanded to know what they were going to do to me, but they just laughed. I was frightened and I knew they could see my fear, and I hoped they would take pity on me. But it just seemed to spur them on. Two of them grabbed me and ripped off my dress. I was wearing nothing else, and a third guard put a hand between my legs and slipped his fingers inside my pussy. What surprised me was the fact that I was wet there. For some reason I didn't understand, the rough treatment was actually turning me on!' Calema blushed in the oppressive gloom.

'Anyway,' she went on, 'he pulled his hand away and another guard pushed his fingers into me. I struggled hard. Despite my arousal I was not going to let them take advantage of me, but they seemed to have other ideas.

'The hand was taken away and I was forced to kneel

65

on the edge of the couch with my bottom presented to them in the most crude fashion. I waited for the inevitable touch of a thick cock-head to my pussy lips. But suddenly there was a burning pain as the rope was lashed across my buttocks. I squealed and cursed them loudly. Their response was to whip me again, this time with far more severity. I bit my lip, determined not to cry out again.

'They lashed me across the bottom again and again. The strange thing is, the more they whipped me, the more I craved for the next stroke.'

'I know that feeling,' interrupted Sahria.

'You know it too?' said Calema with undisguised wonder. 'Then you have been beaten?'

'I have been caned. My bottom bears the marks, I am sure, but it is too dark in here for you to see.'

'And did you find pleasure and delight in the pain?'

'Eventually. I orgasmed whilst being thrashed.' Sahria made the announcement proudly.

'So did I!' exclaimed Calema. 'Three times! The guards took it in turn to whip me. Each time I came I screamed out loud. They must have assumed my cries were due to the pain, and it seemed to give them some pleasure.'

'Did they do anything else to you?'

'Not then. When they were exhausted they collapsed on the floor. I remained in the same position and waited for them to take me. I actually wanted to be fucked, and fucked by all of them! I knew my pussy lips were open in invitation and that my arousal would be obvious if they cared to examine me, but they just lay there, as far as I know doing nothing but staring at my stinging backside.

'After some time they used the same rope with which they'd beaten me to tie my hands and feet together, and then got some more lengths of cord and trussed me like a chicken for the pot. I was then made to kneel so that my rump was once more presented to their gaze. At last, I thought, they were going to fuck me. I have never been so ready to be impaled as I was at that moment. Instead, however, they just left me. They left the guardhouse laughing and joking and slammed the door behind them. I was furious.

'I tried to move but couldn't. I began to feel ridiculous, kneeling on the floor, tied up and with my bottom sticking in the air. My rear was still stinging quite badly, but the pain seemed to compensate for my frustration.

'After some time the door opened again. The guards had returned. They were still laughing like idiots and their breath smelled of ale. I looked over my shoulder and glared at them. One of them took up a long spear, and oh, I thought they were going to kill me! I closed my eyes and braced myself for the blow.

'But instead they forced the spear through my bonds and used it to raise me from the floor, still in my obscene position. Two of them balanced each end on their shoulders and the door was flung open. I was carried out like an animal into the square. There were people everywhere – people I knew. I have never felt so humiliated. The men carried me slowly through the jeering crowd as if purposefully displaying me as their prize. Hands groped my nether regions and fingers prodded inside me. I saw the faces of slaves whom I had abused in the past. Their elation at seeing me in my shame both sickened and excited me.

'I was taken to the palace. As they walked down the long passageways we passed many more soldiers, all of who took the opportunity to finger my private parts. At last, we reached the door to one of the royal chambers. By this time I was shaking with lust and could feel the juices running from me. I must have presented quite a sight.

'The door opened and I was carried in. I managed to look up, and saw a man seated on the edge of the bed. I recognised him immediately. It was Sarne, the handsome prince who so besotted you when he first visited the palace. Do you remember him? He seemed to have quite an effect on you at the time.'

'Sarne?' said Sahria quickly. 'You were taken to the prince?'

'Yes,' replied Calema. 'So, you must know it is he who has taken over the kingdom.' Calema regarded her quizzically. 'Oh, my dearest friend, you are jealous!'

'Nonsense!' snapped Sahria. 'Go on with your story, and leave nothing out.'

Calema smiled knowingly and then continued with her tale. 'I was lowered to the floor and the spear was removed from the ropes. All I could do was kneel there with my hands tied behind my back and my bottom still jutting upwards. I felt so demeaned and so ashamed to be in such a ludicrous pose in the presence of a prince. I tried to move in order to roll over onto my side, but the way I had been trussed prevented this. I looked up at the prince. It hurt my neck, but I wanted to look into his eyes. He simply stared back at me. I remember thinking how cruel his expression was. There was no compassion, no pity for me in my wretched state.

'He stood up and his cloak fell open. I gasped when I saw his magnificent cock. It hung limply from his bushy groin, but even in that flaccid condition it was longer and thicker than the largest weapon I had seen before! I couldn't stop myself from imagining how wonderful it would be to accommodate such a monster. I pictured it long and hard, jutting upward from his chiselled body, ready to impale me to the hilt. My pussy was already wet due to the whipping, and the glorious subjugation of my bondage, but now it itched for sexual contact. I remember thinking that, no matter how big the prince's tool, it would slide into me without the slightest difficulty.'

'And did he fuck you, Calema?' Sahria asked anxiously. 'Did he fuck you?'

'Wait,' teased her friend, 'you are too eager. There is more to my story.

'The prince walked behind me. I looked over my shoulder for a moment and saw him staring at my bottom. I knew he couldn't fail to see the open lips of my sex, and possibly even the other little hole. I looked back down at the floor in anger and shame. Even if a prince, I thought, he should not stare at me in such a lewd and lascivious manner.

'He spoke for the first time. His voice was soft but there was no warmth in his tone. "Such a perfect arse," he said, simply. I was furious! I wanted to respond, to show my anger. I wanted to tell him that he had no business addressing a member of the royal household in such a way, but I decided to keep quiet. I knew that any protest would be pointless. "You have been marked well," he continued. I felt him touch the scorched flesh of my bottom with his fingertips, and I sighed involuntarily. He ran a finger down the cleft between my buttocks until the tip touched my anus. At first I instinctively tightened the sphincter, but then relaxed, and he eased his finger into me. There was no need for lubrication. He slid his finger out again then slipped two, or maybe three inside me. "Ah, sweet princess," he said, "I sense that you are well versed in anal delights." He turned and twisted his fingers inside my bottom until my inner muscles became completely relaxed. He eased out of me and then rose to his feet. I knelt silently, my anus throbbing gently. I heard Sarne move and watched him as he walked past me towards the bed.

'He stood for a moment with his back to me, and then removed his cloak and tossed it onto the bed. I savoured the sight of his strong back, his tight bottom and his long, muscular legs. He turned sideways and just stood there. It became rapidly clear to me that he was holding the pose on purpose. His cock was now fully erect. It jutted monstrously upward. I remember you telling me that the prince was magnificently endowed, but I was unprepared for this. It was plainly too thick for me to circle with my fingers and I imagined that it would surely tear me apart should it enter my pussy. But despite my fears, I have never wanted anything so badly in my life!

'He walked over to a small cabinet and opened the

door. He took something from within and then turned to me. At first my gaze was still transfixed by his huge prick, but then I saw that he was holding a leather tawse. My heart leapt and my mind was filled with a mixture of fear and excitement, and I begged him not to beat me too severely.

'He slapped the tawse loudly on the palm of his hand. "Silence!" he barked. "Your pert flesh is well striped but you will discover that the kiss of the tawse will give you a far different sensation of pain and delight. Your bottom must burn before I take you.'

'Did he,' gasped Sahria breathlessly, 'did he take you?'

'Wait,' teased Calema again, 'you will find out.'

'I can't wait,' laughed Sahria, but inside she was burning with envy. 'Please, please go on.'

'The prince moved behind me. I watched in fascination as he walked, his big cock waving about like a spear. I closed my eyes and clenched my buttocks. I felt him touch my bottom with the tawse and he gently stroked my skin with the harsh leather. He traced the shape of my rear then ran the tip of the tawse between my buttocks until it touched my pussy. He rubbed the full flatness of the implement against my soaking lips. I thrust my bottom out as much as I could in my shackled state to allow him easier access. He coated the tawse with my juices and then moved from me. I was nearly crying with lust.

'The first stroke came without warning. I heard the wet slap and then felt the searing, satisfying sensation of joyous pain. The second stroke was administered almost immediately. The surge of sensation between my legs was such that I knew I would come the next time he hit me. The tawse lashed across both my buttocks with equal force, and the sound of my punishment echoed in my ears like the music of angels. My pussy felt like it was on fire as I climaxed with a violence I had never experienced before. I'd been fucked three or possibly four times earlier that day and had savoured three further orgasms when beaten by the guards, but this was something quite, quite different.

'I cried out in sheer joy as the tawse stung my burning flesh again and again. My entire body was shaking and every stroke caused my desire to increase. I lost count of the number of times my poor bottom was lashed. And it didn't matter; I wanted it to go on forever.

'I heard Sarne toss the tawse to the floor and I sobbed with disappointment. I peered over my shoulder and looked at his face. I was crying, but I knew my eyes were filled with lust. The prince moved to kneel at my side and took hold of his enormous cock by the root. Leaning forward, he stroked my stinging buttocks with the long, thick shaft. Then suddenly he whipped me with it! He actually lashed me with his stiff cock! The pain was insignificant but the knowledge of what he was doing drove me once more to the brink of blissful release.

'He whacked me again and again with it. I don't know if it hurt him to do it, but he was plainly enjoying himself, by the look on his face. The sensation was strangely soothing, albeit highly erotic.

'Presently, he rose and walked back to the cabinet.

This time he took out a small silver jug. He poured some oil into the palm of his hand and rubbed it over his thick cock. He moved back behind me and I felt him pour the oil into the cleft between my buttocks. It felt cool and soothing. I wanted him to massage the fluid over my stinging bottom, but instead I felt him once more ease his fingers into my tight little sphincter. His intentions were now all too clear.'

'Oh, I don't believe it,' Sahria whispered excitedly, the breath catching in her throat. 'He didn't...' She gripped herself between her legs and fingered her erect little bud. The very thought that her young friend could be impaled in such a way by Prince Sarne's magnificent weapon was filling her with disbelief and seething jealousy.

Calema laughed girlishly. She was clearly enjoying Sahria's discomfort. 'The oil eased and opened me more and more, although I was terrified at the thought of what was about to happen. The idea of his superb tool entering my pussy was frightening enough, but *there*, I would have thought it impossible. I turned my head to look back at him. "Please, my lord, I am a virgin in that place," I lied. "You are too big. The pain will be too much." Sarne just sneered at me contemptuously as he continued to push his fingers in and out of my bottom. He poured on some more oil and then eased all four fingers and his thumb into me. I groaned, this time with pleasure. He pushed forward until, incredibly, my tight sphincter gripped his wrist. He turned his fist inside me whilst pouring yet more oil onto my cleft. I remember thinking that it might not be so bad after all. I have always enjoyed the feeling of a thick cock moving in and out of my backside although, of course, I had never experienced one of such magnificent proportions.

'At last he removed his fist from within me, gripped my buttocks tightly with both hands, and tugged them apart. I gritted my teeth. I felt the bulbous head of his cock touch my anus. I took a deep breath and held the air deep in my lungs. I sensed the head move inside me and I gasped. There was no pain – he had prepared me well. He moved forward and slipped about three or four inches into me, then held still. I could feel the monster throbbing within my tight sheath, and I prayed he hadn't come. I wanted more – much more.

'He withdrew slightly and I thought he'd finished, but then he pushed forward again. He forced at least twice the length inside me this time. The feeling of fullness was amazing. There was a slight pain but that soon subsided. He pushed again, and at last he was inside me completely. I could feel his thick bush of hair pressed against my beaten bottom. He held himself still again and the monster throbbed heavily. Then he began to fuck me; he fucked me up the arse with his enormous cock!'

Calema hissed the last few words through clenched teeth. Even in the semi-darkness, Sahria could see that her expression was a picture of delight. Her friend took a moment to savour the pleasurable memory, and then continued.

'My initial fears and the subsequent delightful feeling as he entered me had caused me to forget that I was trussed up. I fought against my bonds, wanting to respond to his incessant thrusts by jerking my body against him, but movement was virtually impossible. I clenched my buttocks tightly. I knew from experience that this would cause my anus to grip him firmly. He groaned and began to move faster. He was ramming his stalk in and out of me without a thought for my discomfort, but I was loving every moment. I gasped and panted for air as he hammered into me, and my pussy ached for release. Suddenly I was coming. I raised my head and let out a blood-curdling scream as my orgasm tore through my loins. The prince responded by thrusting ever harder and, incredibly I came again, even before the first wave of feelings had subsided!

'The prince eased out of me and moved to kneel at my head. His long rod glistened with the oil, the angry, purple end inches from my face. I arched my neck and he moved towards me. I licked the end and then took the plum-sized head into my mouth. I could taste my scent, and I loved it. I could never have imagined doing such a thing before, but in my totally subservient position it seemed utterly right. I suckled him voraciously, my saliva dripping from my chin while he rubbed his long stalk with both hands.

'Suddenly, without warning he roared like a stuck bear and thrust his cock forward so that it filled my mouth. I wanted to swallow his full length down my throat but knew that such a thing was out of the question. The thick stalk throbbed heavily between my lips and against my tongue. I tasted the saltiness of his cream and swallowed hard. He continued to pump rapidly, filling my mouth with more and more of his warm fluid until, at last he was sated.

'He sat back and looked at me. I smiled and allowed a trace of sperm to slip from the corner of my mouth. Presently he stood up and donned his cloak, then clapped his hands loudly. The guards entered immediately. He barked out his orders to them. "Take this vixen to the black chamber, and see that Rapite thrashes her for her impertinence!' I couldn't believe that he could be so cruel, but his attitude seemed oddly fitting, in a strange way.'

The two of them sat in silence for some minutes. Sahria mulled over Calema's fantastic story. She conjured up the image of her naked friend lying roped on the floor with Sarne's huge weapon delving into her most intimate orifice. She was envious, that was true, but she was also happy that the girl had enjoyed such delightful pleasure. It did, however, appear odd to her that the younger girl had often enjoyed the sensations of anal sex whilst she herself had never participated in such deviations. She vowed that it would not be long before she, too, had given herself to this ultimate experience.

She also considered it strange that both she and Calema should enjoy the pleasures of being soundly whipped or beaten. Often in the past men had begged her for more when she lashed their bare buttocks with the most vicious whips. Perhaps all men and women were the same, she mused. Perhaps all were happy to succumb to the delights of pain, if they did but know it.

'We must ally ourselves with the prince,' she said presently.

'What do you mean?' asked Calema.

'We have both learned much in these past few hours. I am sure that Prince Sarne and his cohorts have much more to teach us, and I know that we will both be very willing pupils. I also know that we probably have much knowledge to offer to them in return. Between us we can create the most sexually aware court in the entire world!

Chapter Four

'I want you to tie me to the frame.'

Sahria had spoken suddenly, causing Calema to be startled. 'Certainly, sister, but why?' she said.

'Rapite left me strapped and hanging there. He will be furious if he returns and finds that I am free, and will undoubtedly blame you and punish you most severely.'

Calema laughed coquettishly. 'I don't mind,' she pouted.

'Possibly not, but if we are to persuade him to take us to the prince so that we can put forward our plan, we need him to be on our side.' She took Calema's arm and led her through the relative darkness to the frame. Suddenly the familiar sound of bolts being withdrawn came from the other side of the heavy door. 'We are too late!' exclaimed Sahria. The door opened and the two girls shielded their eyes from the brightness of the torchlight. The squat, shadowy figure of Rapite appeared in the doorway.

'So, you have dared to release your companion from her bonds!' he barked as he fixed the torches to two brackets set in the wall.

'No!' said Sahria quickly. 'It was I who—'

'Silence!' growled Rapite, as he shuffled towards them. He glared at Calema as she stood cowering before him, shivering in her naked vulnerability. He reached out with a gnarled hand and stroked one of her breasts, and then squeezed the nipple spitefully. Calema squealed with the pain, and he laughed cruelly. He groped the other breast.

'Such firm little tits,' he growled, 'and such lovely nipples. I shall have much pleasure piercing them.'

Calema's eyes widened in horror. 'What do you mean?' she asked, her voice shaking with her terror.

'You will see,' he said, as he squeezed her other nipple tightly, causing her to wince. 'The pain will be worth it, I promise.'

'No!' exclaimed Sahria. 'She is too young. Take me, and do what you will with my body, but do not harm my friend.'

'It is all right, Sahria,' protested Calema, 'I will take the pain.'

Sahria looked earnestly at her friend, but Calema's expression was one of abject lust and it was immediately clear that the idea of following Sahria's example and of having her flesh pierced appealed to the younger girl. Rapite continued to fondle Calema's firm flesh, occasionally pinching and twisting her erect nipple and making her gasp with pain and delight. Eventually he tired of his game and moved to stand before Sahria.

He cupped one of her breasts in each hand and raised them. Sahria merely stood proudly still, arching her back slightly to accentuate the size of them. Rapite bent his head forward and took one of her nipple-rings into his mouth, and tugged it sharply with his teeth. It hurt, but she managed not to show her discomfort.

'Be assured, princess,' he sneered, 'these succulent

mounds will be further pierced and chained in the most restrictive of fashions, so that the slightest movement will cause the most exquisite pain.'

'Please, sister, do not argue with our master,' begged Calema, as she took her arm gently. 'I have always longed to have such adornments, and not only in my nipples.' She glanced pointedly down at the tiny rings piercing Sahria's sex lips.

'Be warned, it can hurt,' Sahria whispered, but Calema merely smiled, making it patently obvious that such a prospect didn't concern her in the slightest.

Rapite laughed raucously and slapped Calema soundly on the bottom. 'The little bitch craves pain! I will have much sport with her!'

Sahria realised at once the truth of his words. Whilst she herself had taken much pleasure in her subjugation, Calema's desires appeared to be much deeper, as though she had become a veritable slave to torture and humiliation. She felt a dampness between her legs and knew that she envied her. She smiled at her friend and nodded briefly, then glanced down at the loathsome Rapite, who was now suckling her nipple hungrily.

'Take us to the prince,' she said boldly, 'we have a proposition to put to him.'

Rapite let her breast fall away from his lips and looked at her questioningly. 'Proposition?' he grunted. 'What proposition?'

'It is for the prince's ears only,' Sahria insisted.

Rapite glared into her eyes. Sahria caught the aroma of his foul breath and turned her face away. 'Take care, princess,' he snarled, 'or you will taste the whip and believe me, you will not find its kiss as pleasurable as the cut of the cane!'

Sahria looked back at him contemptuously. They both stared into the other's eyes for some moments, as if each was trying to break the other's will.

Calema broke the uneasy silence. 'Please, my lord Rapite, take us to Prince Sarne and afterwards you may pierce me in any way that pleases you.'

He swung round angrily. 'Once again you appear to forget,' he spat, 'that you are both my prisoners! I can do with you as I wish!'

Sahria rested a hand on his muscular shoulder. 'But surely, my lord,' she whispered, 'is it not better if we are totally suppliant? Would you not prefer it if we gave ourselves completely of our own will, offering our bodies to whatever debasement you should choose to inflict upon us?'

He eyed her suspiciously, but her words seemed to have the right effect. 'You would give yourself entirely?' he wheezed. 'Both of you?'

Sahria shrugged. 'As you have so often said, my lord Rapite, we have no choice.'

Rapite leered at her and jabbed a hand between her legs. He pushed his fingers into the soft, wet flesh. 'Why do you dribble so, princess?' he muttered.

Sahria didn't want to admit that her arousal was the result of Calema's erotic tale. 'It is your masterful presence that makes it weep, my lord,' she said. She reached out and grasped his thick cock through his loincloth. 'It appears that my friend and I have had a similar effect on you.'

Rapite pushed her hand away and moved quickly

towards the open door. 'I will speak to the prince,' he said, 'but heaven help you if this is some form of trickery.' With that he was gone and the door was once again slammed and bolted into place.

'At least we have the torches,' said Calema, after a few moments.

'Let me look at you,' said Sahria, taking her by the arm, 'turn around.' Calema turned her back to her and Sahria bent to examine her tortured bottom. 'You are badly bruised but the skin is not broken. It will heal quickly.' She sat back on the cot and watched as Calema walked around the dank cell, looking in wonder at the array of whips, flails and canes that festooned the walls. She took down a particularly vicious looking bullwhip and caressed the thick lash with the tenderness of a lover stroking a hardening penis.

'Nobody could take a beating from an implement such as this,' she said with awe.

'You would be surprised just how much a strong man can take,' replied Sahria with a grin. Calema replaced the whip and sat next to her friend.

'I had heard tales of this place, but this was your domain and I was never permitted to enter.'

'You never showed any real interest,' Sahria pointed out. 'You were always too busy with the soldiers or the labourers in the fields.'

Calema smiled. 'I could never understand the pleasure in giving or receiving pain. Until now, that is.'

'Would you wish to administer punishment yourself?'

'I'm not sure. I don't think so. I think I would rather *be* punished.'

'Is it the pain that you enjoy?'

Calema thought for a moment. 'Partly,' she answered, 'but it is also the feeling of total helplessness. When the guards trussed me up I wanted them to fuck me, but when they merely lashed me with the rope I came as violently as at any time in the past when I had a lover's rod deep within me. It was because I couldn't move, I think. All I could do was to kneel there with my bottom presented to them. It was as though I took pleasure in my shame.'

'Do you remember Mistress Cale?' Sahria spoke the name with reverence. Calema nodded. 'Do you remember, then, how she would come to our bedrooms after the day's schooling and would punish us for our childish misdemeanours? Some of the things she did to me drove me wild.'

'I think I must have been too young, probably only sixteen or seventeen years old.' said Calema ruefully. 'She would spank me on my bare bottom and that was often wonderful, but that was all. What did she do to you?'

Sahria sat back and drew her legs up against her breasts and wrapped her arms tightly around her ankles. She smiled, her eyes glinting. 'I don't know if I should tell you,' she teased.

'Oh, please,' begged the other, 'please tell me.'

Sahria paused for a moment and enjoyed the flushed look of youthful excitement and curiosity on Calema's face.

'All right,' she said at last. 'I remember one time,

just after my seventeenth birthday…'

'Had you been initiated, like I was?' interrupted Calema.

'Oh yes. My virginity had been taken by the vizier in just the same manner as happened to you. He was followed by twenty of the most handsome nobles in the court.'

'I only had fifteen,' protested the younger girl.

Sahria grinned. 'I think you will find the count was twenty. It is the custom. You probably lost count.'

Calema shrugged. 'Possibly,' she said quietly. 'Go on with your story.'

'I was enjoying a delightful time with two young soldiers in my bedroom. I knew it was forbidden to consort with such lowly types, but they were beautiful and had such fine strong bodies. My initiation had left me with a taste for good hard sex, and I would take it wherever and whenever I could.'

'I know exactly what you mean,' murmured Calema, her eyes glazing over as she pondered recent memories.

'I was kneeling on my bed with one of the soldiers pumping into me from behind as I sucked the rod of his colleague. Suddenly the door burst open and I heard the dreadful sound of Mistress Cale's voice. "What is this?" she demanded, "these men are common soldiers. Remove yourself from them!"

'I was in such a state of sexual arousal that I remained motionless for a brief moment. Mistress Cale grabbed hold of the two men and forcibly pulled them from me. I turned to kneel on the bed and looked at her face. She was furious and I knew I was in for a most severe punishment. My pussy was already running with my juices, but the thought of receiving a whipping excited me even more.

'The two soldiers stood at the side of the bed, trembling like cowards. Their cocks hung limply between their legs, still large but no longer threatening. They were obviously terrified.

Mistress Cale glared at them and barked, "Be gone with you!" and they were away in an instant, leaving their clothing strewn around my bedroom floor. I have often wondered how they would have explained their predicament if they were seen rushing naked through the palace corridors!

'When they were gone Mistress Cale closed the door quietly and turned to face me. For a moment I hung my head in shame, but then I looked up and held her stare; after all, I *was* a princess!

'I was determined not to show any fear, but I couldn't stop trembling, more from lust than terror. She smiled cruelly, obviously thinking I was frightened of her. I asked what she was going to do to me, and my voice sounded like that of a timid child. She walked over to me and grabbed the hair on the back of my head, and yanked it back. She put her face so close to mine that I could smell her stale breath. I tried to turn my face away but she tugged my hair and forced me to look into her eyes. They were blazing with fury. "You know it is forbidden for men such as those to savour the delights of a royal body!" she snarled. "You will be punished in the most severe manner! Do you understand?"

'I said nothing and she yanked my hair again harshly,

causing me to yelp with the pain. "I said, do you understand?" she demanded. I mouthed the word "yes", but barely a sound came from my lips. She threw me back on the bed and stomped towards the door, opened it, and then stopped and looked round at me. "I am going to fetch my little teaser," she said, then disappeared from the room.

'I knew what she meant. Her "little teaser" was a vicious tawse made from the roughest leather. I had encountered its kiss only once before, when she discovered me fondling myself one lonely night, and I knew the pain would be great.

'I began to feel afraid. The times when she had spanked my bare rump with her hand were secretly pleasurable, but the teaser hurt dreadfully.

'My first thought was to refuse to allow her to punish me and to order her from my sight, but I knew she was strong and would easily be able to force me to submit. Then I considered fleeing my room, but again I knew she would find me eventually and that my punishment would be all the more severe. I decided to wait, and to let her do her worst. If I resisted there was a chance she might tell the king, and the soldiers whom I had been enjoying would most certainly be put to death. I didn't want that on my conscience; they had such lovely cocks.

'So I lay on my bed in silent acquiescence, waiting for Mistress Cale to return. Her room was only a short walk from mine, and yet she was taking a very long time. It was obvious that she was making me wait on purpose, making me suffer the agonies of expectation. She knew I had experienced her teaser before and that

I would be trembling with fear and lust. She was deliberately doing it – making me wait. I imagined her to be standing on the other side of my door, clutching and caressing her vicious tawse. I could visualise her stroking the harsh leather, and I suddenly realised that I desperately wanted to feel it lashing across my bare bottom. In my mind's eye I could see the ridges and the splits in the leather and sense the roughness of its texture. The more I thought about it the hotter I became. I wanted it; I wanted it badly. I needed to feel the searing pain of the first blow and hear the thwack echoing in my ears as it lashed across my poor, delicate skin.

'Still she made me wait. I lay on my back with my legs apart and my fingers dipping into the soaking lips of my pussy. I pressed my knuckles firmly against my clit and rubbed myself harder and harder. I turned over so that I was kneeling on the bed with my bottom waving in the air and my fingers still clawing at my oozing sex lips. Why didn't she come to me? Why didn't she fling the door open and lash me until I screamed?

'I pushed my fingers deep inside and then smoothed my juices over the cheeks of my bottom. I knew it would look good; I knew my unblemished skin would glisten invitingly in the candlelight. I dipped my fingers into my hot little pussy again and then brought them to my mouth. I licked my cream from my fingers. It tasted sweeter than any wine. I began to wonder if Mistress Cale's juices would taste so nice.

'I rubbed myself again, this time concentrating on my erect bud. I knew I would come at any moment, and was actually crying with lust. I thought of my two soldier lovers and of how well they had serviced me with their cocks. I needed them to come back to me. I wanted them so badly that I felt I would explode with frustration.

'Suddenly the door opened. I was still kneeling on the bed with my bottom presented to the intruder in the most blatant and obscene manner. My heart was pounding in my chest and I was panting for breath. I looked over my shoulder, and Mistress Cale was standing behind me. She was naked, save for a pair of black leather boots that stretched to just below her crotch. The bush of dark hair between her legs was thick and luxuriant, the curls shining with wetness. She was holding her teaser. I stared at the tawse and began to tremble. There was no fear in my mind, no terror of the pain that was to come – just pure, unadulterated lust.

'She moved to stand at my side and regarded me contemptuously whilst stroking the tawse across her fingers. "Well, princess," she said, "it seems you are more than ready for your punishment."

'She raised one leg and rested her foot on the bed, close to my face. I could smell the scent of her leather boot and found the odour intoxicating. I glanced up at her crotch. The lips of her pussy were open and inviting. She was clearly very highly aroused. There was a long silence, and I watched as a sliver of her juice slipped from within the engorged flesh and trailed slowly down to her foot, looking for all the world like the silk from a spider as it builds its web. For some reason the sight of her vulnerability gave me new courage. I bent my head towards her and licked her cream from her boot. The taste was exquisite.

'I looked up at her, hoping to see some sign of delight within her normally sour expression, but there was none. I glanced back at her crotch. I wanted to bury my face in the soft folds of her cunt. I had never felt that way for one of my own sex before. Thoughts of my two male lovers, and even the tawse, were momentarily dismissed from my mind. After all, she had come to me virtually naked. Surely there was more in her mind than merely a thrashing?

'She reached over and touched my bare bottom with the tips of her fingers. I wanted her to slip them within the folds of my slippery opening, but she merely smoothed the palm of her hand over my plump globes. Her breathing was heavy and laboured. I turned my face away from her and licked the toe of her boot again, savouring the acrid taste of the leather. This seemed to please her. She stood erect while I traced the shape of her foot with my tongue, then moved her foot away and presented me with the other boot.

'I licked obediently. I licked upwards, over her ankle to her calf. Her breathing was becoming even more stilted. I moved higher and circled her knee with the tip of my tongue, then higher still until I lapped hungrily at her thigh. I breathed deeply and the scent of her arousal filled my nostrils. I began to finger myself as I moved my face ever closer to my ultimate goal. I don't know what I was thinking; my mind was racing. The thought of touching another woman in a sexual way would previously have repulsed me and yet, here I was, fully intending to lick the saturated flesh between her legs!

'The tip of my tongue found the smoothness of her bare skin at the top of the boot. I stopped for a moment; for some reason I felt I had gone too far. I looked up at her face. She seemed like a giant, towering above me. Her expression was cold but unthreatening. I licked her thigh again and then moved my body forward. My mouth was less than an inch from her pussy. I remember wondering how many cocks had slipped between those lush folds of sex flesh. I took another deep breath. Her scent was strong but fresh, the scent of a real woman.

'Suddenly she grabbed me by the hair and rammed my face against her groin so that my mouth was pressed hard against her cunt. I began to lick her immediately. She circled her hips and gripped my hair tightly, moaning softly to herself. I pushed my tongue inside her as far as it would go and then moved it in and out like a little prick. Her juices filled my mouth as I suckled her. Her taste was divine. I swallowed avidly and then drank more from her. I drew her outer lips between my teeth and chewed them gently, at the same time delving my tongue between them.

'She leant forward over me and gripped my bottom, still grinding her crotch against my face. I felt the stiff bud of her clitoris against my tongue. I raised my head slightly and drew the little button between my teeth and pressed my jaw hard against her mound. I flicked the tip of my tongue rapidly across her clit. She groaned loudly and dug her fingernails into the firm flesh of my bottom. I licked her even faster, up and down and from side to side. It seemed to come naturally to me.

'Suddenly she squealed and clawed at my buttocks. Her pussy lips appeared to open even wider and my face became soaked with her juices as she came to a shattering climax. I continued to lick her whilst gripping her leather-clad thighs with both hands. I rubbed my face against her soft wet sex lips and lapped hungrily. I licked, probed and suckled her juicy flesh until she could take no more. Eventually she pushed me away and staggered over to sit on a nearby stool. She was panting like a galloping horse, her breasts heaving and her legs trembling.

'I sat on the edge of the bed and looked at her. Although a large woman, she was very attractive for someone of her age. Her fine body was covered in sweat that trickled down over her skin in tiny rivulets, and she was still clutching the tawse. I couldn't believe it – surely she wasn't going to punish me now, not after I had given her such intense joy with my tongue?

'She seemed to read my thoughts. "Well, princess," she said, in the most menacing way, "now your punishment will be doubled!" I asked her why; hadn't I pleased her? But she just sneered and stood up, slapping the teaser against the side of one leather boot. "Not only do I find you allowing your royal body to be impaled by common soldiers, but you then have the temerity to seduce me! Is there no end to your debauchery?"

'I pleaded with her, begged her, but it was all in vain. I no longer craved the pain of the tawse; I wanted gentle, loving sex. I yearned for her to put her mouth to me and to lick me in the same way I had pleased her, but she clearly had other things on her mind.

"Place a pillow under your hips and lie on your stomach, princess," she ordered. I obeyed immediately. "Spread your legs!" she barked. I opened my legs until my toes gripped the two opposite edges of the wide bed and gripped the iron bedstead tightly with my fingers. My bottom was slightly raised by the pillow, which was rapidly becoming wet with my juices. I buried my face resignedly in the other pillow and awaited my punishment.

'I felt her stroke my bottom again with her fingertips. "Such a perfect bottom," she said, "it's a shame that soon it will be marked and bruised." She ran her fingers in the cleft between my buttocks and touched my anus, which made me jump. She eased her fingertip inside the little hole. It hurt, and I cried out. "Ah," she muttered, "a virgin there, it appears." I said nothing. Thankfully, she removed her finger from me and stroked my bottom again.

'Then I felt the tawse being gently dragged across my skin. I could feel the gnarled ridges and could sense the hardness of the leather. I shivered uncontrollably, something that Mistress Cale could not have failed to notice. But she said nothing, and instead tapped my bottom with the teaser. "Such ripe, delicious flesh," she said quietly, almost to herself.

'She moved behind me and I felt her kneel on the bed between my legs, and then she parted my buttocks with her thumbs. There was a long pause, and I strained my neck and squinted over my shoulder. She was staring at my bottom and licking her lips. From the expression on her face it was clear that she was savouring the sight of my virgin hole. I turned my head and pressed my face against the pillow once more. There was something incongruously exciting in what she was doing, although I couldn't explain it. It was as though I was taking pleasure in this basest of subjugation.

'Nothing more happened for what seemed like an age. She just knelt there, studying my behind. I could hear the sounds of the palace from the other side of the door. I heard a group of soldiers marching along the corridor and couldn't help wondering what they might have thought had they seen their princess in such a predicament.

'Mistress Cale must have moved her face closer, for I could feel her warm breath against my bottom. Then suddenly I felt her kiss me, a gentle kiss at the top of the valley between my buttocks. I held my breath, wondering what she was going to do next. Was this a precursor to the beating I was about to undergo? She kissed me again, a little lower this time, and then I felt her tongue sliding wetly along the crease. She moved the tip up and down, allowing it to progress ever lower. I thrust my buttocks upward and felt her part the cheeks further with her thumbs. Her tongue reached the spot just above my little hole. I raised my groin from the pillow completely and thrust my bottom up as if offering myself to her.

'I *was* offering myself to her!

'I desperately wanted her to lick me – there, in that special place.

'She teased me unmercifully, licking around my tight little anus but never once allowing her tongue to touch me there. I could feel the wetness of her saliva dribbling down over the little hole to mix with the juices that seemed to be seeping from my pussy. I began to tremble with lust again. I realise now that this was all part of her game of torment but then, in my innocence, I thought she really was going to lick my bottom fully. And oh, how I wanted her to!

'She drew back after giving me a playful kiss between my buttocks. I lowered myself down on the pillow again, bitterly disappointed. The pillow was wet, a clear testament to the strength of my arousal. I lay in silence for some minutes as she resumed her posture behind me and stared once more at my bottom. My disappointment was rapidly turning to anger. I had satisfied her, I had sated her with my tongue, and yet all she did was tease me.

'I began to wonder just what it would be like to feel a warm wet tongue slipping and sliding over my anus, and even probing inside, and the very idea made me squirm. I vowed that I would demand such treatment from my next lover, whoever it may be.

'Suddenly my thoughtful meandering was cruelly interrupted by a loud thwacking sound as leather hit soft skin, and a searing pain tore through my poor bottom. There had been no warning, not even the drawing of breath from my tormentor. The suddenness of her assault caused me to cry out and wriggle over the bed as though to escape. "Lie down, princess!" commanded my torturer. "Take your punishment willingly or the king will hear what his sweet daughter has been up to this day!"

'I had no choice. The king would be furious if he heard I'd consorted with soldiers and, worse still, if

Mistress Cale told him what I'd done with her. No doubt she would weave a convincing tale of how I'd seduced her through wiles, or ordered her compliance. The painful stinging sensation in my bottom was increasing in intensity rather than decreasing, and I wasn't sure how much punishment I could take. Nevertheless, I moved back down the bed to my original position with the pillow under my groin and my bottom offered to her delectation.

'The second stroke came almost immediately. The sound rang in my ears but the pain didn't seem quite as bad as the first. A third stroke was administered and it seemed as if my tortured skin was becoming numb. There was a long pause. I waited, barely daring to breathe. I knew that three lashes would not be sufficient to satisfy my cruel mistress. My bottom burned incredibly. The stinging continued to increase in intensity the longer I lay there, as the nerves in my flesh once more became alive to sensation.

'The fourth stroke came as suddenly as the first. I yelped with pain as the tawse hit me across the spot where my bottom begins to curve from my thighs. Six or seven more strokes were delivered in quick succession. I don't know exactly how many; I lost count. What was more important was the fact that I was becoming more and more aroused; I could feel a familiar excitement between my legs.

'I had a strong urge to put my fingers to myself in order to relieve some of the pent-up frustration that threatened to erupt from my body, but I thought better of it. I had the feeling that, if I showed any enjoyment in the proceedings, Mistress Cale would merely cease the punishment and leave me to my misery.

'Two more hard strokes were delivered, one to each buttock. I gritted my teeth, I was so close to coming I felt that one more kiss of the teaser and I would go over the edge.

'Mistress Cale walked to stand by my side. I raised my head and looked at her. Tears were streaming from my eyes, but they were tears of lust and frustration. For the first time that day she smiled. "Have you had enough, princess?" she said, quietly. The smile turned quickly into a smirk and I realised that she knew. The bitch had seen that I was about to come and had purposely stopped the beating. My mind raced. I knew that if I begged her for more she would ignore my entreaties, but could I be convincing enough? Could I make her believe that I genuinely didn't want her to continue thrashing me?

'I nodded and spoke weakly. "Yes mistress," I mumbled, "I cannot take any more. My poor bottom stings so." She smiled again, but this time it was a sneering smile. She moved back to stand behind me. "Then perhaps a few more," she said triumphantly. I buried my face in the pillow, anxious that she should not notice my delight at her words. She stood quietly for a moment, tormenting me as usual, then I heard her draw a deep breath. I stiffened my buttocks. I was coming! I just needed the touch of the tawse and it would be complete.

'The leather hit my bottom with such ferocity that I screamed with the pain, but the fire and agony that burned my tortured flesh mellowed rapidly as the full force of my orgasm tore through my loins. I squealed again and writhed on the bed, grinding my crotch against the saturated pillow. The blissful orgasm seemed to last for ages; it was as if time stood still as a million tiny needles jabbed into by little clit at the same time.

'Eventually I relaxed and looked fearfully at Mistress Cale, who was clearly furious. She ordered me to kneel with my bottom thrust high. I couldn't understand it; she obviously knew that further punishment would merely delight me all the more, and yet she seemed intent on continuing. I certainly wasn't going to offer her any argument!

'I knelt as she demanded with my back dipped, and I rested on my shoulders so that my bottom jutted high. She ordered me to part my legs, which I was happy to do, assuming she would no doubt wish to stare at my anus and sex once more – but I was wrong.

'I looked over my shoulder and watched her raise the tawse high above her head. She really was going to thrash me some more! My pussy twitched again. I braced myself for further pain and delight. The tawse swished down and, to my shock the leather whacked fully onto my wet sex. The pain was excruciating! Mistress Cale whipped me twice more in exactly the same place until I collapsed forward onto the bed. This time my tears were for real. My pussy throbbed awfully and every second the stinging got worse and worse. I rolled over onto my back and clutched myself between the legs with both hands. I pressed the palms hard against the wet flesh and it seemed to help ease the pain. I glared at Mistress Cale and, for once she appeared concerned that she'd gone too far. She threw the tawse onto the bed and quickly left the room, slamming the door behind her.

'Gradually the pain subsided and was replaced by a pleasant pulsing, deep within the slippery flesh. I stiffened my buttocks and the throbbing seemed to increase in intensity. I could feel my little bud hardening. I touched myself, then began to rub.

'Just then the door opened and Mistress Cale returned. She was now draped in a diaphanous dress and was carrying a small bronze jug. She sat at the foot of the bed and poured some liquid onto the palm of her hand, then reached forward and smoothed the cool oil onto my abused pussy. She was clearly worried that she had hurt me badly, and wasn't ready for my response to her gentle caress. I came with a sudden wail and gripped her hand with both of mine to force her to press hard against my pulsating mound. She tried to pull her hand away, but I found a strength within me that could not be overcome. I rubbed my cunt against the bitch's palm until I was completely sated, and then I let her go, dismissing her from the room with a contemptuous wave of my arm.

'I lay still for a few minutes, pondering on what had happened to me, and how much pleasure I had achieved from the experience of pain. Soon after, as I lay there in a dreamy state, the door opened and my two lovely soldiers slipped into my bedroom.

'And this time I bade them lock the door.'

Chapter Five

'I wish that evil clown Rapite would hurry up,' said Calema, in a hushed tone. 'I'm feeling cold.'

Sahria slipped her arm around her naked friend's shoulders and hugged her tightly. Their jailer had been gone for at least an hour, possibly more. Time seemed to have little meaning within the confines of their dark, dank prison. 'Let's just hope he has kept his word and spoken to the prince,' she whispered, more to herself than to her young companion.

They sat in silence for a while. Occasionally one of the torches spat angrily as the tallow sparked momentarily, but other than this the only sounds that could be heard were those of the two female's steady breathing.

Calema was the first to break the deathly hush. 'Do you think Prince Sarne will allow us to join him?' she said.

'I hope so,' replied Sahria. 'I feel there is much that we can offer him, and there is certainly much that he can teach us.'

Calema suddenly burst into tears and buried her face in Sahria's bosom. 'I don't want to die,' she sobbed. Sahria stroked her head gently, caressing the soft blonde tresses lovingly.

'You won't die,' she whispered. 'The prince has tasted your sweet body. He will want more.'

Calema sat up and looked directly into Sahria's eyes. She seemed so young, so vulnerable. Sahria wanted to kiss away her pain and fear. She hugged her again and closed her eyes. She imagined Calema kneeling on the floor of the palace with the prince plunging his enormous tool in and out of her bottom, and she felt very envious. He *had* to agree to their terms and, more importantly, she knew that she had to feel that same monstrous weapon within her own clutching sheath.

The sounds of the door bolts being withdrawn made them both jump. The door creaked open and Rapite entered. He stood still for a moment, his muscular frame a silhouette against the bright light of the passageway behind him. Sahria and Calema rose to their feet.

'You are to come with me,' he snapped at last. 'The prince will see you.'

Sahria walked slowly over to him. She couldn't help but notice the way he leered at her breasts as they swayed provocatively with her movements. 'May we not be dressed in some way, to preserve our dignity?' she asked, as she stood before him. 'A simple robe would do.' She did her best to hold a regal pose and glared down at him, but his lecherous gaze remained fixed on her breasts, and to her profound annoyance she sensed her nipples hardening. She mentally cursed her lack of self-control.

Calema stood next to her and Rapite glanced across at her smaller, pert breasts, and smiled. 'I must fuck you on your return,' he chuckled, 'but come now, the prince will not be kept waiting.'

'What about clothing?' demanded Sahria, choosing

to ignore his arrogance.

Rapite eyed her contemptuously. 'Don't be ridiculous!' he barked, then turned his back on the two girls and strode out of the room. Two burly guards stood in the doorway, waiting patiently, so Sahria looked at Calema and shrugged.

'We can't stay here,' she said. 'We might just as well go and see what the prince wants of us.' They stepped out into the corridor, both blinking in the strong torchlight. Rapite was already disappeared around a corner at the far end of the hallway, and they followed his direction quickly.

The two girls passed numerous groups of soldiers on their long walk to the throne room. The men leered at their nakedness and joked amongst themselves. Sahria was aware that they had all probably seen them naked before, but that had been under very different circumstances. It was they who would have been the prisoners, bound and gagged and more than willing to succumb as victims to their tortuous demands.

One of the soldiers grinned broadly as they approached him and raised his skirt to reveal his naked genitals. Sahria eyed the drooping member dispassionately, and then looked across at her friend. Calema's expression showed that she had more than a little interest in the proffered specimen. 'Come, sister,' Sahria snapped, 'the prince awaits us.'

Calema tore her gaze from the man and the two girls strode purposefully after the scuttling form of Rapite, and caught up with him just as he entered the throne room. They stood in the doorway, waiting to be summoned. Prince Sarne sat lazily on the throne with one leg resting over the arm of the great chair. A woman knelt at his feet, the movement of her head betraying the fact that she was paying oral homage to his huge weapon.

Presently the prince noticed Sahria and Calema in the doorway and clapped his hands together. The girl at his feet immediately moved away and Sahria caught a glimpse of his magnificent erection, before he pulled his cloak across his nakedness. She felt an immediate twinge of desire between her thighs, and knew that whatever the prince demanded of her would be given happily.

'Come forward!' he barked. Rapite scurried ahead of them towards the prince with his head bowed. Sahria strode slowly forward with her head held high, in order to maintain as much dignity as was possible in her naked state. Calema followed suit, until the two women stood at the base of the step to the throne.

'Do you not bow before your prince?' Sarne rose to his feet as he spoke. Sahria remained unmoving. The prince stepped down and stood in front of her, his face barely inches from hers. He reached forward and cupped and raised her breasts in his hands. 'Such luscious mounds of delight,' he continued. 'I wonder how many strong hands have kneaded this soft flesh and how many mouths have suckled on these hard nipples.' He pinched her stiff buds simultaneously, and then released her firm breasts.

He turned to face Calema. The young girl bowed her head, more in fear than in reverence. 'And what of you, princess?' he said. 'Is your bottom still aching?'

Calema's face coloured with her embarrassment.

'You are a pig, Sarne,' snapped Sahria protectively, and regretted her impertinence immediately and feared that she had gone too far. The prince swung round and glared at her. She held his stare, determined not to show him that she was terrified. He reached out and pinched one of her nipples and twisted it until she winced with the pain. Still she looked straight into his eyes, unblinking and without emotion. The prince's expression softened and he released his grip. Sahria breathed deeply as she felt the blood pumping through her breast. He stroked it gently, and Sahria glanced down and noticed the shape of his erection pushing against the heavy material of his cloak. She felt an inner sense of relief; he may hurt her and that would be fine, but he wouldn't kill her. He wanted her as much as she wanted him.

Sarne stepped back up to the throne and sat down. 'My friend here, Rapite, tells me you have a proposition to put to me,' he said in an arrogant tone.

'Indeed, my lord,' replied Sahria.

'Speak then.'

Sahria paused in order to give her words some effect. She looked around the room at the sea of faces of the peasants and soldiers who were leering unashamedly at her and her beautiful friend, and how she hated them!

She looked back at the prince. His hand was tucked under his cloak and he was clearly masturbating.

'Calema and I are well versed in all matters sexual,' she began.

'That is well known,' the prince interrupted, with a

wry laugh. He looked around proudly at the assembled throng and they immediately joined him in his derision with forced hoots of laughter. Sahria managed to smile.

'We feel it would be to all our benefit if we shared our knowledge,' she continued. 'There is nothing on the subjects of subjugation and humiliation that we do not know. Let us recruit and train young girls to do your bidding, and I promise that there will be more pleasures for you than you could ever have imagined.'

Sarne stroked his chin thoughtfully. 'And what would you achieve for yourself by doing this?' he asked.

'All we ask is the freedom to enjoy the company of men as we always have done. We will, of course, willingly take our punishment whenever we exceed the boundaries of what is permitted, my lord.' She bowed subserviently as she spoke these last few words, and there was a long pause.

'Where will you find these women?' asked the prince at last.

'We will send messengers throughout the country. Once word is out that the handsome Prince of Persia is seeking concubines it is certain that many girls will flock to the court.'

Sarne smiled, and Sahria felt a deep sense of satisfaction. She had wisely surmised that the key to the prince's heart was to be found hidden within his monstrous vanity. He clapped his hands and laughed loudly. 'Let it be so!' he called to the court. 'Forthwith Sahria and Calema are to be known as the Princesses of Pleasure!'

A rousing cheer rang around the great room, but

Sarne looked into Sahria's eyes and his expression darkened. 'Know this,' he said in a hushed tone, 'should you or your protégées displease me in any way, your punishment will be most severe!'

'We will willingly, nay gladly, accept the pain, my lord,' Sahria replied. 'But there is one more thing I wish to ask of you.'

'Speak.'

Sahria looked pointedly at the impressive bulge at the front of his cloak. She spoke quietly, anxious that no one heard her words other than the prince. 'You have promised that you will fuck me. You have already taken my dear friend here in a way that I have never experienced with any man. I ask that soon you will pleasure me in the same manner.'

Sarne smiled cruelly. 'When I am ready…' he whispered. 'When I am ready.'

'Spend one night with me, Sarne, and I promise it will be a night you will never forget.' Sahria had never begged for sex before; to do so was totally alien to her nature, and yet here in front of a host of people she was demeaning herself willingly. She was trembling, the lust for this powerful man burning inside her.

'You go too far, princess.' Sarne was clearly angry. 'I am your prince, and you will address me as such. Furthermore, you will never again demand my attention. Is that clear?'

Sahria nodded, a tear forming in the corner of one eye. 'Yes, my lord,' she said meekly. She looked up into his face. 'Am I to be punished for my impertinence?' She chose her words carefully, and the prince seemed impressed by her sudden subservience.

'Indeed you are,' he said. 'In one hour you will be taken to the marketplace trussed up like a stuck pig and there, well, you will see.'

Sahria looked into his face, her eyes shining. 'Will it hurt, my lord?' she asked.

'It will.'

'Thank you, my lord.' Sahria bowed her head and saw that his penis was now jutting from within the folds of his cloak. The head was purple and damp with his own juices. She wanted to fling herself forward and take the monster into her mouth and suckle him again, but she resisted the temptation. Sarne covered himself and stood up.

'Rapite,' he barked, 'take these two to the blue chambers. That will be their home.' He dismissed Sahria and Calema with a nonchalant wave of his hand, and the two girls followed Rapite from the room.

The princess and her friend had both known about the blue chambers of course, but had never any reason to visit them. When Sahria's father ruled the country the blue chambers were the quarters of the royal concubines. These were women who were blessed with the utmost beauty and who were skilled in all manner of deviance. Their purpose was to give pleasure to the king and his chosen guests. Sahria had always found the concubines to be a somewhat surly group, with ideas well above their class. The simple fact that they had allowed the royal penis to penetrate their luscious bodies seemed to give them the opinion that they were superior to lesser members of the court. She had little to do with them, unless they joined her in her own games. Even then, she usually felt uncomfortable with their arrogance and their self-opinionated posturing.

When she and Calema arrived at the chambers they found them empty. Sahria immediately wondered where the royal concubines had been taken. Surely Prince Sarne would want to savour such a cornucopia of beauty for himself? She turned to Rapite, intending to question him as to the girls' whereabouts, but the small man was already leaving the room having obediently completed his escorting duties. The door was closed firmly behind him and Sahria heard the now familiar sound of bolts sliding into place.

The rooms were opulent, but the two girls knew they were still prisoners. Sahria sat heavily on one of the many couches and clasped her hands between her thighs. She stared gloomily at the rich carpet, hearing Calema opening various drawers and cupboards.

'By Allah, look at this!' she heard her friend exclaim. Looking up, she saw that the girl was holding what seemed to be a most un-feminine pair of pants. They were large and black and seemed to be made of a kind of soft shining leather.

'They don't look very nice,' she said.

Calema held the garment out excitedly. 'No, no,' she giggled, 'look inside them!'

Sahria stood up, took the pants, looked inside, and laughed loudly. Within the tight, sensuous material were sown two perfectly shaped phallic rods, each the size and proportion of an average male penis. The material itself felt strangely soft, but not like leather at all. Sahria put the garment to her face and sniffed.

Rubber! She had only come across the new material once before in her life, but had never forgotten its sensuous aroma. She breathed deeply. The scent was intoxicating. She fondled the two phalluses. They were hard but supple in her grip, their purpose obvious.

'Let me try them,' said Calema excitedly.

Sahria grinned and handed the garment to her friend. 'You'll need some lubrication,' she laughed. Calema immediately searched amongst an array of coloured bottles on a nearby table until she found what she wanted.

'This should do,' she said, as she poured a little of the viscous liquid onto the palm of her hand. Sahria held the pants open while her friend rubbed a liberal amount of the oil over the rigid black stalks. Calema's eyes were shining and her face was flushed. She poured some more of the fluid into her hand and then slipped her fingers between her legs. Sahria watched as she oiled and prepared her tight little sphincter, pushing two, then three fingers inside to open herself in readiness. Calema looked up at her and grinned. There was no shame or embarrassment in her expression. In fact, it became abundantly clear that she was actually enjoying being watched as she slipped her fingers in and out of herself.

The downy hair covering her pussy was glossed and matted. It was quite evident that there was no need to lubricate this other sheath. Calema took hold of the pants and carefully stepped into them. She pulled slowly up her shapely legs, all the time grinning broadly, then hauled them higher until they fitted snugly around her hips. Sahria couldn't see what was happening, but could tell from the expression on Calema's face and the girl's heavy breathing that the two rods were entering her slippery sheaths. Calema pulled the pants up fully and then reached between her legs to push them hard against her crotch, so that the phalluses filled her two holes completely.

The girl stood erect, and then walked slowly around the room. 'It feels fantastic!' she sighed. 'They move slightly when you walk. It's like being fucked in the cunt and the arse at the same time!'

'Have you ever done that – for real, I mean?' asked Sahria, a little taken aback by the strength of the girl's obscenities.

Calema cocked her head to one side and looked at her friend questioningly. 'Of course,' she said, 'haven't you?'

'No, I told you, I've never been fu… I mean, I've never taken it in my bottom.'

'Oh yes, sorry, I forgot. It really is the most wonderful experience, especially if the man's blessed with a large weapon.'

'So you said,' responded Sahria, with unconcealed envy. 'I'm sure that soon I will discover the delights of such deviations.'

'Perhaps it will be sooner than you think,' said Calema wryly. 'Who knows what's going to happen to you in the marketplace.'

Sahria sensed a familiar twitch within the folds of her pussy as her nerves tingled with the excitement of the unknown. She was fully aware that she would be bound, or trussed up like a stuck pig as the prince had described it, and he had promised that it would hurt –

but the marketplace? Why would she be taken to such an open and public area?

She watched as Calema tried on other items of intimate clothing, some erotic, others simply beautiful. The rubber pants were discarded in favour of more feminine underwear, items made of silk and gossamer, each exotically revealing in its own way. The royal courtesans certainly knew how to please their lovers visually.

There was a loud rap at the door and two burly soldiers entered, followed by a woman whom Sahria had not seen before. She was tall, even taller than Sahria, and was as broad as any man. She wore a coarse horsehair tunic and long voluminous pants, which did nothing to flatter her stout body, and she was carrying a number of ropes of varying thickness. Sahria eyed the ropes hungrily, certain that they were for her.

'I am Jama,' proclaimed the women in a loud, husky voice. 'I am bid by the prince to prepare you for the marketplace. Which one of you is Princess Sahria?'

Sahria stood up and bowed meekly. 'I am she,' she said, quietly.

The big woman walked up to her and grasped her by the wrists. She tugged her arms apart roughly and held them above her head while she stared unashamedly at Sahria's superb breasts.

'Fine tits,' Jama announced, with the tone of a vendor in a slave market, 'and the nipples are already pierced.' She looked down. 'The cunt-lips too… I like that!'

Sahria saw her lick her lips and began to feel more than a little concerned. It was true that she enjoyed

110

the company of her own sex occasionally, but there was something innately repulsive about this manly creature.

Jama forced her to turn around by twisting her wrists painfully, and then pushed her forward so that she fell against the couch with her elbows resting on the cushions. Sahria felt the woman grip her hips and raise her until her legs were straight and her bottom was presented obscenely.

'Such a superb arse!' exclaimed Jama. 'It is perfect for the purpose I have in mind!'

Sahria felt her pawing the smooth bruised globes of her buttocks and, despite her feelings of revulsion, began to sense a strong desire for more intimate physical contact.

Jama eased a finger into her anus. 'So tight! I will need to cream it well or the pain will be too severe!'

With these words Sahria became certain that her final virginity would be lost that day. She felt the lips of her pussy opening and her juices beginning to coat the insides of her thighs. She was both afraid and excited at one and the same time. Jama started to move her finger in and out of the tiny hole, and Sahria trembled visibly.

'Do you like that, princess?' The big woman spoke in an almost kind tone. Sahria nodded, but Jama laughed cruelly and pulled her finger from within her then slapped her hard on the bottom. 'Time to prepare you!' she barked.

Sahria stood erect and waited obediently while Jama sorted through the array of ropes. Calema was sitting on another of the couches, and was watching the proceedings intently. She was naked again and was gently, almost nonchalantly, pulling at the wet lips between her legs with the fingers of one hand, while caressing the bud of her clitoris with the other. Sahria considered that she might be remembering her own time, when she had been trussed and abused by the guards.

Jama ordered Sahria to lie on the floor on her back. She obeyed immediately. The guards were looking at her intently, clearly savouring the sight of her voluptuous body. Their erections jutted under their loose skirts, two fine cocks that at any other time she would have suckled on voraciously. Her pussy ached. She knew that whatever happened to her in the marketplace she would be happy if someone, anyone, fucked her.

Jama knelt by her side and forced Sahria's legs back until her knees were pressed hard against the cushion of her breasts. Jama squatted across her and sat heavily on her thighs to hold her in this position, while deftly binding her ankles together with a coarse length of rope. Then, with equal finesse, she bound her wrists to her ankles and tugged the rope tightly before looping it around the back of Sahria's neck and knotting it once more around her feet.

Further lengths of rope secured her elbows to her knees. Sahria was then pulled forward so that she sat in a painfully awkward position on her bottom and then, while one of the guards held her steady, Jama threaded a final piece of thick rope around her back and under her knees, knotting it against her spine.

The big woman stood up and examined her work

proudly. Sahria struggled against the bonds, but knew escape was impossible. She could barely move a finger.

Jama nodded to one of the guards, and he produced some sort of black garment, which looked similar to the phallic pants Calema had so enjoyed. Jama took the garment and knelt once more at her side, and Sahria could now see that it was some sort of hood made from the same exotic material as the pants. There was just one hole, approximately two inches in diameter, cut in the centre.

Jama stretched the garment and quickly pulled it over Sahria's head. Although tight, the rubber felt comfortable, like a second skin. The hole was positioned over her mouth so that breathing, although difficult, was not impossible. The material was totally impervious to light and Sahria realised that, for the duration of her punishment, she would be blind. The thought both terrified and thrilled her.

She felt herself being pushed onto her back again. The heavy knot pressed against her spine and hurt her, but she knew it was pointless to struggle. The next thing she felt was the sensation of fingers stroking and probing the wet lips of her pussy. Now she understood; the torment of being abused and unable to move due to her bonds would be heightened a hundred-fold by not being able to see what was happening or, indeed, who was abusing her.

A greased finger was pushed into her anus up to the knuckle. It hurt a little at first, but gradually the muscles of her sphincter became used to the intrusion and relaxed. The finger was removed and then replaced by two, the oil easing their passage remarkably. She moaned softly, and heard Jama speak.

'Relax, sweet princess, I said I would prepare you.' The fingers were removed and then Sahria felt an intense pressure against her rear hole. 'Four fingers now, princess,' said Jama huskily. Sahria inhaled sharply as her hole was stretched expertly. There was virtually no discomfort, just a remarkable sensation of fullness.

'How does it feel, Sahria?' It was Calema's voice, drifting into her consciousness like part of a dream.

'Good,' Sahria replied, 'very good.' Her throat felt dry as she spoke and the strong scent of the rubber was making her head swim. She felt more oil being poured onto her bottom, and then the fingers were turned and twisted inside her. Jama pushed hard, and Sahria suddenly realised that her entire hand had entered her forbidden sheath. She groaned. It was uncomfortable in the extreme, but incredibly erotic. She could sense the muscles of her sphincter gripping the woman's thick wrist as Jama twisted her fist deep within her. More oil soaked her buttocks and the hand was pushed further and further inside. Sahria groaned loudly. The delightful repletion she felt was marred only by the feeling of emptiness within her other aching sheath.

Jama began to fuck her bottom with what felt to Sahria like the full length of her forearm. She moved it steadily in and out with a gentle curving motion. There was still no pain for Sahria, and her only discomfort was the fierce pressure of the knot against her back. She could feel her juices slipping from the engorged lips of her pussy, and knew she was close to coming. She began to gasp for breath and moaned over and over again with each forward thrust. She wanted to buck her hips in response to the delightful if unusual intrusion, but she was unable to move. The ropes seemed to tighten as she headed towards her inevitable climax. The coarse hemp dug into her flesh painfully, the agony merely serving to heighten her pleasure.

She felt Jama plunging her fist rapidly in and out. Her clitoris felt like it was ready to burst. She stiffened her thigh-muscles and held her breath, and the orgasm hit her like an explosion of fire, tearing through her lower body with an unstoppable force. Sahria screamed, and she heard Jama laugh. The fist was plunged even faster and Sahria screamed again, this time in delightful agony.

Slowly, the throbbing within her bud subsided and the hand was eased from the tight confines of her plundered bottom. She was sweating profusely. The rubber hood felt distinctly uncomfortable against the hot skin of her face. She felt someone wiping the oil from her buttocks with a soft damp cloth, and enjoyed its soothing touch. The knot dug against her spine, and she was grateful when gently moved to lie on her side.

Nobody spoke for some time. Sahria wondered what lay in store for her. Her bottom ached, but the feeling was not unpleasant. She thought it strange that she should have had such a violent orgasm without the slightest touch to her clitoris. She wondered if the guards had enjoyed the show. Perhaps they had been standing over her, masturbating while her poor backside was invaded in such a base manner.

She wanted their cocks. She wanted them inside her pussy and her mouth right now. Surely they would not be able to hold back after such an erotic demonstration. But perhaps they too had come; perhaps their cream had joined with the oil to lubricate Jama's thick wrist. Sahria wanted desperately to have the hood ripped from her head so she could see the two men and discover whether or not their erections still stood proudly.

Then she heard the familiar sound of Calema moaning softly. Something was happening to her friend – something pleasurable. Then she heard the equally recognisable sound of skin slapping against skin. Calema was being fucked! One, or maybe both of the guards were sating their lust on the younger girl. Although happy for her friend, Sahria was angry and frustrated. Calema's whimpers became steady groans of ecstasy, and Sahria felt like sobbing.

'Calema,' she cried out. 'Tell me what's happening!'

'I am being fucked, sister,' was the simple reply.

'Tell me in detail, so that I can picture your joy in my mind!'

At first all she heard was the sound of Calema panting steadily, coupled with the distinctly male groans of her lovers. Then the girl spoke, her words taking on the rhythm of her lovemaking. 'I-am-sitting-on-a-lovely… *fat-cock*.' Calema gasped the words with some apparent difficulty. Sahria heard her take a deep breath and then she spoke again, her voice a little more controlled. 'It is deep inside me, moving up and down.'

'Where is it?' demanded Sahria. 'In your pussy?'

'No, it's in my bottom. The other one is in my pussy.'

Sahria pictured the sight of the delicious girl sandwiched between the bodies of the muscular soldiers. 'Keep talking, Calema,' she begged.

'I can't, it's too difficult,' she groaned. 'Oh, by Allah's beard they are both so big!' The wet slap of groin against groin grew louder and more rapid. Sahria longed to block the sound from her ears, then suddenly Calema shrieked with delight as her orgasm took hold of her. Sahria heard the couch creaking loudly and felt she would die of frustration.

'Jama,' she ordered, perhaps unwisely, 'bid one of the guards to come to me.'

'It is too late,' panted Calema, 'they've both come inside me!'

Sahria rolled over onto her back with a supreme effort, and felt the knot bite into her spine. She stiffened her limbs and forced herself against the ropes that bound her so tightly. The coarse bonds bit into her flesh, sending anguishing jabs of pain throughout her body, and then, to her delight she felt the touch of a thick cockhead against her soaking sex lips. It appeared that one of the soldiers had not been quite as sated as her friend had supposed.

'Oh, by Allah, I don't believe it,' Calema spoke with a hushed, excited voice.

'What is it?' demanded Sahria. 'What is happening to you?'

'It is not me… it is you,' the girl said in wonderment.

'What do you mean?' panted Sahria, as she felt the

thick rod delve deeper into her aching sheath.

'It's Jama. She – she has a penis! She is both a man and a woman at the same time!'

Barely had the words been spoken when Sahria felt the incongruous touch of a wet pussy pressing against her bottom as the thick cock filled her own hot cunt. A she-male! She had heard of such unfortunates before, but had never encountered one.

And now she had one inside her!

Jama rammed the full length of her cock deep into Sahria's juicy honeypot and held herself still. Sahria could feel the wetness of the she-male's cunt against her bottom, and could sense the juices flowing between her buttocks to soothe her aching anus. Despite her initial shock at being penetrated by a she-male, she began to respond by gripping the rod tightly with her vaginal muscles.

She gripped it as tight as she could with her pussy lips and Jama began to thrust in and out of her. The sensation was so unusual and so mind-blowingly erotic that Sahria quickly began her inexorable climb to blissful release. Jama continued to pump into her steadily, occasionally allowing her rod to slip from the silky grasp of Sahria's sex, and to rub their pussies together before once more sliding the stiff pole back into the warmth of her sheath.

Sahria tensed her groin once more to grip the thrusting rod as tightly as she could, wishing her hands were free to fondle the wet sex lips and humping buttocks. Suddenly she heard Jama take a gasp of breath, and then heard the she-male squeal, and the sounds of her lover's joy brought Sahria over the edge, too. The two crashed together as they orgasmed, grinding their pussies together until they could stand no more.

Jama slipped the still erect rod from within Sahria and moved away, and Sahria rolled onto her side, gasping for air.

She sensed that Jama had risen to her feet. 'I feel you are now well prepared,' said the she-male. 'It is time to take you to the marketplace.'

Sahria felt herself being raised from the floor, no doubt suspended in a similar way to that described by Calema earlier. Then they were moving out of the room, down the corridor and towards the palace doors.

Chapter Six

Sahria felt the cool of the evening breeze brush against her naked skin, and knew she was being carried out into the open. She was hanging by her ankles and wrists from some sort of wooden staff that was being carried by the two burly soldiers who had so recently impaled her beautiful young friend. Her body swung heavily like that of a dead animal, and her limbs ached.

She heard the sound of voices, many voices coming from all around her. The noise grew into a babble as the faceless crowd seemed to draw nearer. Sahria felt herself being positioned between some form of supports, and she was left hanging naked and helpless in front of the cackling rabble. They were very near to her now; she could smell the sweat on the peasants' filthy bodies, and could almost taste their stale breath on her lips. They were laughing and jeering at her. Sahria felt an overwhelming sense of hatred for them, and for the prince for putting her in this humiliating position.

How could this be happening? How was it that she, a princess no less, could find herself trussed up and hanging, naked and hooded in the presence of the scum of the marketplace? She struggled vainly against her bonds and the coarse rope dug into her tender flesh. Her pathetic efforts caused the crowd to jeer all the more. Sahria suddenly felt a deep sense of shame, knowing that this crowd of lowlifes was staring at her nakedness, no doubt each one feasting his or her eyes on her breasts, the lips of her pussy, and even *that other place*.

How proud they must feel, she thought to herself, gazing at her obscene display, and looking lustfully at the sex of a royal personage!

She heard a strong clap of hands, and then Jama spoke. 'People of the market, pray silence for the Princess Sahria!' A great cheer rose from the crowd, followed by more laughter and jeers. 'The noble Prince Sarne has decreed that the princess must be punished for her impertinence! You, the people of the city, will deliver the punishment!'

A second, far more raucous cheer rang out from the crowd. Sahria struggled again, but in vain. She was terrified. The peasants would surely kill her to avenge her past cruelties.

Jama spoke again. 'The princess will hang here for one hour. During this time you may use and abuse her body at will, but do not wound her in any way, nor cause her blood to flow. Sate yourselves with her luscious body, fill her every orifice with your seed, and whip her soundly so that she knows the meaning of true pain!'

There was a long silence, and then somewhere in the distance a dog barked. Sahria hung helplessly, her heart pounding. She knew that all she could do was wait and hope that the people would not be too severe in their vengeance.

The shaft from which her body hung creaked with her weight. She thought of them all leering at her, and imagined a thousand pairs of peasant eyes drooling over her, and strangely, found that the thought pleased her. A sliver of her juice slipped from the deep folds of her pussy and trickled down between her buttocks.

Somebody touched her, a cautious caress on one of her buttocks. Another hand stroked one of her breasts, and then another grasped the other. She began to relax under the gentle, almost tender caresses.

'Whip her!' The cry was sudden and was immediately met with a loud cheer.

'Yes, whip her!' echoed another voice, almost manic in its tone.

'And then fuck the bitch senseless!' yelled a third.

Sahria felt the hand stroking her bottom move to cup her sex. 'She's wet,' said a voice.

'Whip her! Whip her!' The cry became a rhythmic chant, rising to a raucous babble as more and more of the crowd joined in.

Then suddenly the noise stopped abruptly.

Sahria was left once more to dangle helplessly alone. She heard a girlish giggle and then felt the rough hand of another tormentor stroke her pussy, and then smooth her creamy juice over her buttocks. Clearly whoever was doing this was well versed in the art of flagellation, for the pain would be all the more intense when the whip was administered to her dampened skin.

She waited, scarcely daring to breathe. The accursed dog barked again. As though taking this as a signal the first stroke came with a suddenness that made her cry out aloud. The rope cut her across both buttocks. The pain tore through her like a knife and she squirmed against her bonds. A second stroke was delivered with equal severity, but she kept silent; Sahria vowed to herself that she would not show pain or fear to this foul rabble again.

More and more strokes were administered, each one slicing expertly across her tortured bottom, not one missing the mark. Sahria sensed her clitoris hardening until it seemed fit to burst. Her juices flowed and her flesh became numb. The lashing of the rope across her bottom became nothing more than sounds, and she yearned for the exquisite pain to return.

A final blow cut her neatly across one buttock, with the knotted end of the rope whipping against the soft wetness of her sex lips. She found the pain intense and delightful. Her little bud throbbed with arousal and her juices continued to seep from within her. She heard the rope thrown to the ground, and felt a deep sense of disappointment. It hadn't been nearly enough.

Once again she felt the gentle caress of the rough hand on her beaten bottom. The fingertips dipped into her soaking pussy and began to circle, as if attempting to open her even more. She sensed that someone was standing close to her face, and lowered her head back as far as the rope tied around her neck would allow. She could smell the scent of a man, sharp but not altogether unpleasant. She realised at once that whoever it might be was standing with his genitals just inches from her face. She opened her mouth expectantly, and almost immediately felt the touch of a bulbous cock-head to her pouting lips. She opened her mouth wide and took the plum-sized knob within, and lapped around its shape with her wet tongue. Within seconds she felt it throb heavily and tasted the familiar texture of a man's cream as it filled her mouth. She swallowed hard, while gripping the pumping stem tightly between her lips.

The man withdrew his rapidly wilting cock from her, only to be replaced by a smaller specimen, which was forced unceremoniously into her mouth until the tip jabbed at the back of her throat. Sahria arched her neck as best she could and swallowed, managing to take much of the length down her throat. The penis was small, probably less than six inches in all, so she was able to accomplish this trick with ease.

The man began to pump his cock in and out of her mouth, seemingly happy that she was able to take his full length, so that balls pressed against her nose each time he pushed forward. Meanwhile, the fingers continued to delve within the soft wet folds of her pussy. Then the fingers moved away and she waited for the inevitable touch of an erection to her sex lips.

But instead she received a crisp slap on her tortured bottom. The shock of the blow was such that her teeth rasped hard against the stalk held deep within her mouth, and the man cried out in pain. But he didn't withdraw. Instead he fucked her mouth rapidly, as though sating his anger as well as his lust. She knew he wouldn't last long at such a pace, and he came quickly, his groin suddenly pressed hard against her face, crushing mercilessly against her as he emptied his balls into her throat. Sahria swallowed heavily, fully aware of the effect her undulating throat would have on her unseen lover.

Her bottom was slapped again, harder this time, then again and again. The stinging blows sent shocks of delight throughout her lower body. She allowed the now flaccid penis to slip from her mouth and then, as she expected, welcomed yet another stiff intruder between her lips and down her throat.

There were more spanks, and then the rope was administered again. The pain of the lash was far more pleasurable to her than the relatively gentle slaps of the hand, and her juices began to flow once more.

She began to think what her poor bottom would look like, striped by the rope and red from the spanking she had received, and the thought excited her immensely. Six more lashes were delivered with the rope. Two of them made contact with her sex lips, the second bringing her to the brink of orgasm. She allowed the man who was fucking her mouth to ease his weapon from her until she was suckling just his cock-head. She wanted to taste his cream, knowing it would be enough to give her the release for which she craved.

She circled his knob with her tongue, purposely licking under the ridge and around the glans, all the time suckling the thick stem with her pouting lips. He came with a roar and his seed jetted over her tongue to the back of her throat. She lapped the sperm greedily, savouring the texture and the taste while continuing to suck hard on the throbbing tool until he had no more to give.

Somebody touched her bottom – just a simple touch, nothing more, but it was enough. With a muffled cry she came; not a strong orgasm but a gentle, welcome release. The man removed his wet cock from her mouth and she gasped for air, finding it difficult to breathe through her nose due to the restrictions of the hood.

Fortunately it was some minutes before another stiff rod was forced between her lips. She was left to hang alone for some moments, and could hear the people moving about, some of them talking under their breath. The sight of their erstwhile princess in such an inappropriate predicament must have filled them with wonder and disbelief.

Presently, the fingers of three or maybe four hands began to paw at her pussy. They tugged at the rings that pierced her soft outer lips, and delved deep inside her. She felt two or three fingers being pushed into the greased sphincter of her bottom. Jama had prepared her well; there was no pain, only pleasure.

Then all the fingers were withdrawn. Somebody gripped her thighs tightly and, at last she felt the welcome intrusion of a long and extremely thick cock entering her sex. She moaned with delight. Her groans became immediately muffled by another rigid stalk being forced into her mouth. Using all her expertise she brought him to orgasm within seconds, and once again swallowed all he had to give.

Not one, but two cocks replaced him. Sahria licked their spongy ends for a few moments, then managed to take just the bulbous heads within her mouth. It was enough for them. They came quickly, rivulets of sperm dripping from her lips and running over the smooth rubber of her hood. The other man, meanwhile, was gently fucking her with long, deep strokes. His fine erection stretched her honeyed depths beautifully, and filled her completely. With each forward thrust the head of his large cock touched her cervix and sent waves of pleasurable sensations throughout her groin, while the thickness of his rod meant it rubbed constantly against her erect clitoris.

He pumped steadily without altering his pace or rhythm. He used every inch of his superb cock, sliding the full length effortlessly into her sheath, withdrawing almost completely until just the tip remained within the grasp of her sex lips, and then thrusting into her until his balls pressed against her wet bottom.

Sahria loved the way the stranger was fucking her. There was no animal urgency; no rapid but all too brief thrusting; just steady and very long strokes. She felt it could go on forever. The crowd was forgotten, as was her discomfort at being suspended by her wrists and ankles. Having a huge prick deep inside her seemed to give her body all the support it needed.

She felt the man run his hands tenderly over her naked body until he cupped her breasts. He pinched the nipples, which caused her to gasp with delight. Then he managed to ease his head between her stretched arms and she felt him bite each nipple in turn. He suckled the engorged buds alternately, occasionally nipping them between his teeth. He worked her breasts expertly, charging her body with new and exciting sensations as he continued to fuck her with the same long strokes.

While he was still sucking one of her breasts Sahria felt him move a hand down her body, until he began to slide his fingers along the cleft between her buttocks. He tickled her anus, and this simple touch made her shiver. Her buttocks were stinging again, the numbness having worn off. The combination of the delightful sensations of sexual intrusion, the hot aching of her bottom, the expert suckling of her nipples, the gentle but totally satisfying way he was fucking her, and now the teasing touch to her well greased anus, was almost too much for her to bear. She longed for someone else to force his cock into her mouth to complete the joy she was experiencing, but for some reason no other peasant touched her.

Sahria began to wonder what her unseen lover looked like. He was clearly a fit man. His thigh muscles felt taut and muscular and his grip of her breasts had been firm, although the skin of his palms had felt unusually soft. Perhaps he was an officer of the guard, unused to manual labour.

But it was his cock that impressed her the most. It was so long and so very thick. Even the prince himself, with his wondrous stalk, would not be able to fill her more. The bud of her clitoris throbbed against the bone-stiff flesh of his magnificent weapon, and Sahria knew she was coming. She began to pant heavily and groan loudly as she neared her climax.

Suddenly, her lover stopped moving and held his stiffness deep within her succulence. Sahria couldn't believe it; she was so close. 'Fuck me…' she begged, 'fuck me hard!' But the stranger ignored her plea and the feelings of impending release subsided. Sahria sighed her frustration, and then he was moving again with the same easy strokes. Yes, she thought, this time… this time…

He stopped again at the crucial moment. He was teasing her in the cruellest manner, and she felt like crying. She ached for release, but he was denying her the ultimate pleasure. He began to fuck her again, and she gripped his rutting pole tightly within her sex flesh. She wasn't going to be denied a third time.

Suddenly her unseen lover began to pound in and out of her like a man possessed. The thick head of his cock hammered against her cervix and his gnarled stem rubbed rapidly against her throbbing button, and she was coming. The fires of joy took control of her senses and she screamed. She screamed again as a second orgasm hit her, then a third, and then a fourth. She had never experienced anything like it before.

Gradually the stranger slowed his movements and then slipped from her. Although fully sated Sahria felt empty, needing more. She vowed to herself that she would discover the identity of her unknown lover and follow him to the ends of the Earth, should he wish it. She felt him run his fingers along the wet cleft between her buttocks, and then she groaned happily as he eased three or possibly four of them into her slippery anus. He twisted and turned his fingers inside her, and she knew. He was going to fuck her there. He was going to force his huge cock into her virgin bottom! Jama had prepared her well, but the prospect still terrified her.

But there was nothing she could do, and that was quite evidently the whole point of the punishment. The once royal princess had to succumb to the basest of humiliations in the presence of the scum of the city, and suddenly she became aware once more of the crowd. They had watched her being whipped and spanked, they had witnessed her take cock after cock into her mouth, and they had seen her being fucked. Now they were about to witness her lose her final dignity.

Sahria knew she would be unable to resist him. The way he probed and turned his hand within her tightness gave her the most pleasant and relaxing of feelings. His exploring fingers felt wonderful inside her, but now she wanted the real thing, and she finally admitted to herself that she needed it badly.

She wasn't to be kept waiting for long. The man removed his fingers and Sahria felt him part her buttocks, and she gasped as his bulbous knob touched her anus, and then took a long deep breath as he began to slip his immense length steadily into her oiled sheath.

Her final virginity had been surrendered, given to an unseen stranger!

In a way she had hoped it would be Prince Sarne to be the first to penetrate her forbidden orifice, in the same way he'd taken Calema. She had imagined herself lying on a royal bed, her body naked and oiled with the scented creams of the orient, and her prince would have taken her while musicians played gentle airs and slaves fanned their sweating bodies.

Instead she was in the marketplace, suspended by her wrists and ankles, having her tortured bottom buggered by a complete stranger in front of a crowd of peasants! And yet, the thought no longer troubled her. Instead, she found it incredibly intoxicating. He was deep inside her now. She could feel his muscular thighs pressing against her buttocks and his balls resting against the cleft. He remained still for some moments as if allowing her to get used to this unnatural intrusion. She breathed gently and savoured the feeling of absolute fullness.

At last he started to gently fuck her bottom with long easy strokes, in the same way that he had delighted her before. The tightness of her grip relaxed and he increased his pace. The wooden pole from which she was hanging creaked as her body swung rhythmically in time with her lover's urgent thrusts.

He moved faster, his thighs slapping noisily against her bottom. Sahria knew he was sating himself this time; there was no tenderness, no concern for her own pleasure. He gripped hold of her narrow waist and began to hammer in and out of her as his fingernails dug into her flesh. His breathing became more and more laboured. His moment was near.

He was pounding against her so hard by now that Sahria feared the frame securing her might break and they would be sent crashing to the ground. The ropes around her wrists and ankles dug into her flesh, and her limbs ached dreadfully, but she didn't want it to end.

Faster and faster he moved until, suddenly he withdrew. She heard the wet slap as he rubbed himself, and then heard him groan and gasp. The hot cream splattered onto her stomach and breasts, and a cheer rang out from the watching crowd. More and more of his juices soaked her skin. Sahria could feel it running in little rivulets down the sides of her body. There seemed to be no end to his release. She wondered what a picture she presented now, hanging naked and coated with sperm.

There was a long pause, then somebody clapped, and Sahria heard footsteps as the crowd began to disperse. Then she felt her hands and feet being untied. She was lowered gently to the ground by strong arms and the remainders of her bonds were removed as she sat down, the coolness of the stone beneath her helping to soothe her bottom.

Finally the hood was dragged, somewhat roughly, from her head. She blinked in the evening sunlight, and gradually her vision cleared. Most of the crowd had gone, leaving just a couple of stragglers who were still enjoying the sight of their naked and abused princess.

Sahria pulled herself stiffly to her feet with the aid of one of the guards, and looked down at her body. Her breasts and stomach were coated with streaks of cooling semen.

'Do you feel that you have been punished sufficiently?' The voice was that of Prince Sarne, and Sahria swung round to see him standing behind her. He was naked, and his cock hung heavily between muscular thighs.

'You!' she exclaimed with sudden comprehension. 'It was you!'

'You seemed to enjoy it,' he replied confidently.

Sahria now realised why none of the peasants had touched her when her well-endowed lover was penetrating her; no one would have dared! She glanced down again at her stained body, and then looked back up at him. 'I must bathe, prince,' she said, with an imploring tone.

Sarne picked up his cloak. Sahria thought for a

moment that he was going to cover her shivering body with it, but he merely wrapped it around himself, and then held out an arm. 'I will escort you back to your chambers,' he said. 'There you may bathe, and then we will speak of your future.'

They walked slowly back to the palace. Sahria limped slightly, her arms and legs still aching from her subjugation, her back stiff.

But most of all her punished bottom ached, and this was the most wonderful feeling of all.

As Sahria lay soaking in the blissfully warm and scented waters of her bath, she mused on the events of the previous days. One minute she had been the most powerful woman in all the kingdom, with slaves at her beck and call, and the next she was to be seen in the filthy marketplace, naked and trussed like an animal. She couldn't help but wonder what the peasants must have thought, seeing her in that predicament, her lashed bottom being impaled by the prince's mighty penis.

She thought about the men who had forced their erections into her mouth, and of how she had willingly swallowed their cream. How they would talk about it in the alehouses tonight! 'Did you see me?' she could hear one of them saying to his cronies as they supped from their filthy mugs. 'I fucked the mouth of Princess Sahria, and she swallowed the lot!'

She allowed a hand to drift in the water and rest between her legs. She playfully caressed her sex lips whilst closing her eyes and breathing in the sweetly scented air. Her bottom still stung, and her pussy and anus still ached as a blissful reminder of the prince's superb intrusion, but she felt good. Despite the humiliation, or possibly *because* of it, the last few hours had seen her enjoy the best sex ever.

Princess of Pleasure, Sarne had dubbed her, and she liked the sound of it. She would find many young girls and teach them the joys of pain and subjugation. She would serve the prince and, in return he would serve her with his wondrous cock.

She heard a noise and looked up. Calema had entered the room and was looking at her with a concerned expression on her face. 'Are you all right?' her friend asked.

'Yes, why?'

'I watched what happened to you; I watched from the window.' Calema moved over to her and sat on the edge of the bath. She was wearing a short diaphanous robe that did little to conceal the curves of her slender body. Sahria thought how attractively vulnerable she appeared.

'Do you ache, you know, down there?' continued Calema.

'My bottom's a little sore, but it is worth it,' Sahria admitted. 'It was the most wonderful experience I've ever enjoyed.'

Calema wet her hands and began to soap Sahria's shoulders and neck, and Sahria lay back and closed her eyes. 'I told you it would be good,' her friend said. 'The first time I took a man in that way I had the most powerful orgasm ever. The head of his cock seemed to touch something deep inside my bottom that caused the tremors of pleasure to surge through me in an instant.'

'It wasn't like that for me,' said Sahria. She sat up to allow Calema to gently wash her breasts. 'It was the stretching and the feeling of fullness that was wonderful, coupled with the fact that I could do nothing to resist. I found my helplessness to be intoxicating.'

'The prince is a very good lover,' continued her friend. She soaped both of Sahria's nipples simultaneously, causing them to stand firmly erect. Sahria closed her eyes again. It was the first time ever that Calema had touched her so intimately, and she liked it – she liked it a lot.

'Would you like me to get in the bath with you?' her friend asked.

Sahria opened her eyes and regarded the girl carefully. Calema smiled and, without waiting for an answer, stood up and removed her robe. She was naked, her small breasts moving gently in time with the pace of her shallow breathing. She held Sahria's gaze as she stepped into the bath, and then she slipped slowly into the creamy water next to her.

Their bodies touched lightly together, Sahria feeling the silky smoothness of Calema's thigh pressing against her own. Calema began to wash her breasts again, but this time she squeezed them while rubbing the palms of her hands against Sahria's erect nipples. 'Sometimes a woman needs gentle lovemaking,' breathed the younger girl.

Sahria looked at her, a half smile playing across her lips. Calema's words and the look of total desire on her face made her intentions quite plain. For a brief moment Sahria felt unsure; they had been naked together many times in the past, they had even shared lovers on numerous occasions, but they had never enjoyed each other's bodies before.

Any doubts that she might have harboured were dismissed forever when Calema moved a hand from her breast, slid it down under the water and cupped her already aroused sex. 'Oh, Calema,' she gasped. She gripped her friend's wrist in a half-hearted attempt to stop her, and then caught her breath as Calema's fingers slipped inside her.

'Shh,' whispered the girl, 'relax and think only of your own pleasure.'

Sahria did as instructed, laying back once more, with her head resting against the rim of the bath and her eyes closed. Calema began to move her fingers gently in and out, worming them against the tender outer lips of her sex. The knuckles rubbed over the erect bud as her fingers danced within her, teasing and opening to allow the warmth of the water to wash against her innermost recesses.

'Oh, Calema, my sweet treasure,' mouthed Sahria, her words husky and barely audible. 'You can have no idea how long it is that I have dreamed of you doing this.'

'I, too,' replied her friend, as she increased the rhythm of her intimate caress.

'Then why have you never approached me in such a way before?'

'It never seemed right, until now.' Calema moved her hand forward and slipped all four fingers deep into Sahria's sex. Sahria gasped loudly as Calema's thumb tickled her button while her fingers wriggled inside her honeypot.

'Do you mean, because I am no longer a princess?' she managed to say.

'You'll always be a princess to me,' breathed her friend.

Sahria turned her face and their mouths met. They pressed their lips together urgently and their tongues darted, searching and probing against each other. Sahria moved her hand between Calema's legs and quickly found her soft pussy, the lips already open and fleshy to the touch. She slipped her other arm around Calema's waist and then managed to cup her pert bottom with her hand. She clutched the girl's nether regions with both hands and tugged her body against her own, their mouths still crushed together in the most passionate kiss that either of them had ever experienced. She could feel Calema's firm breasts rubbing against her own, the nipples as hard as jewels. She rubbed her friend's pussy rapidly, at the same time easing two fingers of her other hand into the tightness of Calema's anus.

Calema pulled her face away sharply. 'I want to lick you,' she gasped.

'And I you,' replied Sahria. With this simple exchange the two girl's clambered out of the scented waters. Sahria lay a thick woollen towel on the floor and lay on it expectantly. Calema stepped over her, the water slipping down her body and dripping onto Sahria's face.

'Sit on me,' Sahria begged. 'Sit on my mouth.'

Calema obeyed immediately. She squatted down

quickly and offered her sweet sensuality to Sahria's waiting tongue. Sahria licked the cleft between her friend's buttocks, and then gazed for a few moments at the beauty of the sight before her hungry eyes. She examined the delicate wet folds of Calema's pussy, framed by a thin fuzz of blonde curls. She had seen it before, of course, but never so close. The flesh was glistening, not with water but with the juices of arousal. It was quite the prettiest vision she had ever seen.

She licked the cleft again and felt Calema lean forward. Sahria raised her parted legs and Calema began to suckle her sex flesh greedily. Sahria gazed at the puckered sphincter of her friend's anus. It was hard to imagine something the size of Prince Sarne's mighty rod slipping comfortably into such a tiny entrance.

It looked too delicious to ignore. She pushed out her tongue and playfully prodded the tip into Calema's bottom. The little entrance relaxed immediately, and Sahria was able to slip the full length of her tongue deep inside the welcoming orifice. She moved her tongue slowly in and out, orally fucking Calema's bottom while her friend happily guzzled her hot pussy.

Sahria allowed her tongue to slip from within Calema's anus and began to concentrate her attention on the girl's juicy cunt. She found the taste to be exquisite, a heady mixture of the scent of the bath and the strong aroma of feminine arousal. She lapped around the outer lips, then drew them into her mouth. She licked between the lips rapidly, ensuring that the tip of her tongue flicked rhythmically against her clitoris at the same time.

Calema's hips began to buck in response. Sahria

knew from her movements that she wouldn't last much longer. She licked faster, pressing her mouth hard against the fleshy cushion of Calema's pussy. The sweet taste of her juice changed suddenly, becoming sharper and even more sensuous. Her friend was coming, and Sahria desperately wanted to share her joy. She felt Calema nip her sensitised bud between her teeth, and that was all she needed. She came suddenly, sensing her fluids of love flowing copiously onto her friend's face at the same time as she drank from Calema's delicious flesh. The two girls groaned and gasped, the sounds muffled as they devoured each other. They rolled over and over, wave after wave of orgasm ripping through their writhing bodies until, at last there was no more.

Sahria and Calema lay in each other's arms for what seemed like an age. To Sahria the marketplace seemed a dim and distant memory, for now there was just one person in her life; just one human being who mattered, and that person was lying next to her, sleeping peacefully.

Chapter Seven

It had been ten days since Prince Sarne conquered the kingdom – ten days of pleasurable instruction. Sahria had used the time well. She had willingly accepted punishments for any minor misdemeanours, and considered that she had charmed the prince with her beauty and grace.

He had listened intently as she related tales of her numerous sexual conquests. Sahria told him every little detail, sparing nothing until she considered that he had learned much of the intricacies of a woman's physical needs. For her part, she discovered that the pleasure she took in the domination of the male was remarkably similar to that enjoyed by the prince himself whenever he indulged his carnal cravings with the girls of the court.

It became abundantly clear, however, that the girls sorely needed to be instructed. They needed to learn the true pleasures of abject subservience if they were to ever satisfy the needs of the prince and his cohorts. This was to be Sahria's task, ably assisted by her young friend and lover, Calema.

There was only one matter that disappointed Sahria. Despite the fact that she invariably wore the most revealing and provocative garments, and notwithstanding her seductive manner whenever she was in the prince's presence, he had not attempted to touch her intimately, let alone carry her to his bedchamber. It was as though the incident in the marketplace had never occurred. She thought about tackling him about it and asking directly if she had displeased him in any way, but decided that silence, at least for the time being, was the wisest course to take.

Today was to be a very special day. Sahria chose her clothing carefully from the array of exotic garments left by the royal courtesans in the blue chamber. She stood in front of the polished mirror and examined her pose critically. She knew that her presentation and demeanour on this day was of the utmost importance. A group of girls had been gathered from the furthest regions and brought to the court by a band of merchants who had heard stories of the prince's requirements. They had expected to sell the girls as slaves, but were quickly disabused of this and sent packing by the royal guard. Now Sahria was to be introduced to the girls as their mistress. The instruction was about to begin.

Sahria chose a long pair of black boots made of soft and shining leather. They had extremely high heels and stretched to about halfway up her smooth thighs. Her sex was completely exposed and was now pierced by six small jewelled studs, which glinted within the folds of her outer lips. Her upper body was tightly encased in a basque made of similar black material, which was drawn in at the waist. Her full breasts were supported by a shelf of stiff leather, expertly woven into the fabric of the garment, the effect being to make them thrust proudly. Between the rings that pierced her nipples she had fixed a thin chain of solid gold.

She wore black leather gloves that reached up her arms, and completed the outfit by donning a brief black mask that just covered her eyes. Her long black hair flowed freely and brushed sensuously against her bottom as she moved.

She picked up a small but vicious whip in a gloved hand and smiled as she took in her reflection. It would be clear to the newly arrived girls that she was someone to be obeyed.

The door to the other bedchamber opened and Calema entered. At least, Sahria assumed it was Calema; at first it was difficult to tell. She was dressed from head to foot in black rubber, the garment forming a second skin which seemed to shine with a luminescence of its own. Holes had been cut for the eyes, nose and mouth, and her pert breasts jutted through the clinging outfit through two more openings, and between her legs, Sahria could see her freshly shaven pussy through another small aperture.

'You look beautiful!' exclaimed Calema, as she walked fully into the room.

'So do you,' Sahria sighed. 'Absolutely beautiful.'

Calema giggled coquettishly at her words. 'I found this outfit in my room,' she said. 'It is made of the same strange material that formed those pants we found – you remember, the ones with the little cocks inside.'

'I remember,' said Sahria. She walked slowly around her friend in order to examine her more closely, and noticed with little surprise, that another hole had been cut in the rubber to reveal Calema's mouth-watering little bottom, and slapped the rounded globes playfully.

'The girls are assembled in the pink chambers,' she continued, 'let's not keep them waiting.'

Calema collected a couple of canes and a small tawse and followed her friend out of the room. They walked slowly down the corridor. The soldiers they passed gave them the expected appreciative leers, but the girls ignored them, keeping their heads held proudly high. Sahria could sense that Calema was nervous by the shallowness of her breathing, and felt somewhat apprehensive herself, but she was painfully aware that she had to show herself as arrogantly confident at her first meeting with her young charges.

Nearing their destination they were met in the passageway by Prince Sarne. He was standing in the doorway of another set of bedchambers, with a pretty girl under each arm. Sahria sensed a pang of jealousy as she looked at the innocent countenances of these nymphets and, although barely out of her teens herself, began to wonder if it was her age that was the reason why he had not approached her again.

'Greetings, my princesses of pleasure,' he said as he bowed before them mockingly. 'Your charges await you. See that they are well prepared.'

'You are not joining us, your highness?' asked Sahria.

The prince grinned and hugged the two girls in his arms tightly. 'I thought I would educate these two myself,' he said with a booming laugh, and the girls giggled nervously as he turned and escorted them into the bedchamber. Sahria watched him go with a benign expression on her face, and then turned to Calema.

'Come,' she said, rather too sharply, 'we have work

to do.'

The pink chambers had once served as the place of rest for the more highly placed servants of the old king, and was comfortably furnished with sofas, beds and fine drapery, all of it in different shades of summer. Neither Sahria nor Calema had ever found the need to enter the chambers before, but now they stood within its simple opulence as servants themselves.

A group of girls sat huddled together in one corner of the main room. There were six of them, each one looking as innocent and vulnerable as the two the prince had selected for pleasurable pursuits. They stared wide-eyed at Sahria and Calema, as they stood before them in their exotic and erotic garb.

'Stand!' barked Sahria.

The girls obeyed immediately, pulling themselves nervously to their feet. 'Come forward and stand before us!'

The girls shuffled towards them clutching each other's hands like frightened children. As they approached, however, Sahria could see that they were anything but children. The merchants had chosen well. Despite their simple white smocks she could see that they all had beautiful and mature bodies. Some were slim and lithe; others were voluptuous and curvaceous. Facially, each one was lovely in her own way. She glanced at Calema. Her friend's eyes were sparkling and she was licking her lips, her penchant for enjoying the touch and taste of those of her own sex clearly apparent.

'I am Princess Sahria, and this is my assistant, whom you will know as Princess Calema.' Sahria spoke the words proudly and smiled as the girls bowed their heads in reverence. 'From this moment you will all address us both as mistress. We are here to teach you, to instruct you in the customs of the court of Prince Sarne, and to prepare you for his pleasure.'

She paused to allow her words to have full effect.

'You are to be trained as royal concubines,' she continued, 'and, who knows, one of you may even rise to become his queen.'

With that the girls broke into excited chatter. 'Silence!' roared Sahria. The babble stopped immediately. She walked along the line and looked closely into their lovely faces. The girls stared dutifully at the floor.

All of them, that is, but one.

She was the last girl to be faced by Sahria. She was tall, almost matching Sahria's height despite being barefoot, and had ebony-black skin and proud Nubian features. Her hair was cut short to the scalp and her huge eyes shone with a mixture of pride and excitement, and she looked directly at Sahria without blinking.

'What are you called?' Sahria asked quietly.

The black girl took a deep breath. 'I am Zia,' she replied, 'and I, too, am a princess.'

'There are no princesses here,' hissed Sahria, 'only servants and free men.'

'You introduced yourself as a princess, and your friend too.'

'Silence!' Sahria glared into the girl's eyes angrily. Her argument was unassailable. Zia's expression remained impassive, almost regal. Sahria quickly

145

realised that she would have to make an example of this one if she were to hold any sway with her other charges.

'Remove your clothing,' she ordered.

'Mistress?' Zia queried.

'Immediately! Do not question my orders or you will feel the lash.' She brandished the whip to emphasise her point, and Zia reached for the hem of her smock and pulled the garment quickly over her head, then let it fall to the floor. Sahria heard Calema gasp at the sight of the naked African. Despite her height there was nothing manly about her shapely form. Her flawless, sable complexion accentuated her womanly contours, her skin shining healthily in the bright morning light that streamed in through the many windows set in the domed ceiling of the chamber.

Sahria walked slowly around her and examined her closely. Her breasts were large and firm, with nipples pointing slightly upward thanks to the conical swell of her fleshy orbs. Her waist was narrow and her stomach flat and smooth. Her belly curved sensuously towards the thick bush between her long legs, and the lips of her sex were barely visible through the lush matt of black hair.

But it was her bottom that was the most appealing feature of her superb body. The firm globes of her buttocks jutted with a pert arrogance that seemed to defy gravity, and appeared to be demanding immediate attention from a lover's hand, tongue or cock. The deep cleft between them was formed like an erotic promise that Sahria knew few men would be able to resist. Knowing Prince Sarne's sexual preferences in this respect, she was surprised that he had not chosen Zia as one of his early morning's sexual companions.

Sahria looked across at Calema. Her friend was staring at the statuesque form and was openly caressing herself between the legs. Sahria turned back to Zia, and could certainly see the attraction. The Nubian exuded sexual promise from every pore.

'Kneel before Mistress Calema,' she ordered, but Zia remained motionless. 'Now!' With an infuriating confidence the black girl walked over and stood in front of Calema. 'Kneel, I said!' barked Sahria.

Zia slowly lowered herself to her knees, keeping her thighs erect so that her face was level with Calema's chest.

'Suck her nipples,' commanded Sahria. There were a few giggles from the group of girls. 'Silence!' she hissed, and the room fell into an immediate hush.

Zia eased forward and took one of Calema's nipples between her thickly pouting lips. Calema groaned softly as the Nubian suckled her.

'Now the other,' ordered Sahria. Zia glanced contemptuously at her, and then did as instructed, and Calema sighed with pleasure. 'Now, bend lower and place your face between her thighs and pay oral homage to her pussy.'

'I will not,' Zia refused defiantly, and Sahria immediately lashed her viciously across the buttocks with her whip. Zia yelled in pain, but made no move to lower herself further. Sahria whipped her bottom again with even greater force than before, but Zia made no more sound. A third lash cut her squarely across both buttocks, and this time the girl fell forward and buried her face between Calema's rubber-clad thighs.

'Is she licking you?' asked Sahria, and Calema shook her head. Once more the whip tore across the quivering black buttocks. 'Lick! Make her come with your tongue or I will thrash you until you bleed!' Sahria then watched with satisfaction as Zia's head began to move up and down, and the room filled with the sounds of sensuous lapping.

She laid the whip on a table and sat on a low couch to enjoy the proceedings. In her kneeling position, Zia's bottom jutted out even more erotically than when she was standing, and Sahria could see the dark promise of her anus and the thick lips of her sex. Four dark red stripes criss-crossed her perfect buttocks as testament to her punishment. Sahria felt an overwhelming desire to crouch behind her and lick the wondrous globes as though to soothe her pain, but thought better of it. She had decided that before any of the girls could enjoy the delights of sex they must all first relish the joys of pain.

Calema closed her eyes and rolled her head from side to side. She was cupping her own breasts and pinching her nipples. Zia's head bobbed faster, and Calema groaned and rested her hands on the girl's shoulders, then raised one leg and pressed her foot on Zia's back. Zia turned her face slightly and Sahria found that she could now see her tongue flicking rapidly against Calema's shaven pussy. She sensed her own sex lips becoming damp and crossed her legs, anxious that the other members of the class should not become aware of her arousal.

She looked at the other girls. Each one was staring

at Zia as she lapped hungrily at Calema's juicy prize. She smiled to herself; this proud African had been subjugated and they had all witnessed her mistress' triumph.

Suddenly Calema squealed as her orgasm tore through her body. She gripped Zia's head and ground her crotch against her face. Zia's head bobbed up and down rapidly again as she devoured the cream that Sahria knew would be filling her mouth. Zia moved her head back, nipping Calema's outer lips between her teeth, and Calema shuddered as a second wave of release hit her. Zia didn't stop her oral ministrations for a moment, and it was obvious to those witnessing her subjugation that for all her earlier protestations she was an expert in the art.

Calema finally pushed her away and fell back to collapse onto a nearby couch, and the girls began to chatter again excitedly. Sahria stood up quickly and clapped her hands, and the room fell into silence once more.

'May I rise, mistress?' Zia asked presently.

'You may,' replied Sahria, enjoying the proud girl's apparent capitulation. The girl pulled herself stiffly to her feet and stood before her, head bowed. Her face shone with Calema's juices, glistening in the sunlight. 'Join the others,' said Sahria quietly. Zia rejoined the line, and Sahria studied her carefully; somehow she no longer bore the gait of a princess.

'You are to tell me your names and detail your sexual experience.' Sahria was standing once more in front of the line of timid girls, addressing them like a tutor would instruct her class. 'You begin, Zia. We already know your name, of course.'

Zia stepped forward. 'I am eighteen years of age and no man has ever taken me.' The group gasped in astonishment.

'I find that difficult to believe, Zia,' said Sahria.

'It is true, mistress. I am… I *was* a princess. My father, the king, would have slain any man who dared to touch me.'

Sahria was delighted; a virgin of such infinite beauty would surely be a prize the prince would be eternally grateful for. 'Have you never yearned for the touch a man?' she asked, and Zia hung her head in embarrassment. 'Speak,' said Sahria, in a softer tone. She had no wish to humiliate the girl further, but her curiosity burned.

The girl nodded. 'The men in my country rarely wore clothing. On the rare occasions that my father was absent the young men of the court would sport themselves deliberately in my sight, teasing me unmercifully. One in particular tempted me. He was handsome, strong and muscular, and possessed the loveliest weapon imaginable. It hung almost to his knee and I had many long nights of painful frustration as I tried to picture it in its full magnificence. But it was not to be.'

'How do you come to be here? If you are a princess, how is it that you were delivered like a slave by a band of common merchants?'

'Soldiers of the Egyptian Pharaoh attacked my home. I escaped with some of my close consorts, but our caravan was captured by the merchants.'

Sahria suddenly felt a pang of sympathy for the girl. 'What became of your father?' she asked carefully. Zia hung her head and she noticed a tear slip down her sable cheek, and knew the answer. She moved to stand before the next girl, anxious to lighten the mood of the proceedings. The girl couldn't have been more different in appearance or demeanour.

'What is your name?' she asked, her voice resuming an authoritarian tone.

'I am Aisha,' the girl said quietly.

'You are Aisha, *mistress*,' commanded Sahria.

'I am Aisha, mistress,' the pretty girl corrected in a hushed tone, her large eyes widening in fearful resignation.

Sahria walked slowly around the trembling figure, stroked her shoulders with the whip, and then ran the tip of the handle down to the hem of her short smock and hooked it under the delicate material, raising it slightly.

'Remove it,' she ordered. The girl quickly pulled the smock over her head and then stood naked before the assembled group, her head bowed in shame. She had a waif-like body with apple-firm breasts, narrow waist and boyish hips. Her skin was as white as alabaster, although the cheeks of her face were flushed with embarrassment. Her hair was long and blonde with barely a curl in the smooth tresses, which cascaded and fell about her slim shoulders, framing the elfin features of her cute face.

Her only similarity with the statuesque Zia was her full, pouting lips, which seemed to be permanently pursed for a long and passionate kiss. 'Look at me,' said Sahria, as she raised the girl's face by lifting her chin with her whip handle. Aisha looked up nervously. Her eyes were wide and clear blue and shone with virginal innocence. 'Tell us about yourself.'

The girl glanced around at the others, then looked at Zia, who nodded in encouragement. 'As I said, mistress, my name is Aisha,' she said. 'I come from the north, where the weather is cold and the countryside is lush and beautiful. I am seventeen years of age. I was captured by a band of rogue fishermen one day whilst walking along the beach near my home, and sold as a slave. My new master tired of me and I was sold again to the merchants who brought me here.'

'Why did your master tire of you?' asked Calema. Aisha looked at the rubber-clad figure sitting on the couch.

'In truth, it was his wife who wanted rid of me,' she answered. 'She was jealous.'

'Did you have sex with your master?' asked Sahria. The girl nodded. 'Yes, mistress, many times.'

'And the wife found out?'

'She was usually there. I... I had sex with her, too.'

Calema rose and sidled beside her, resting a hand on her narrow shoulder. 'Did you enjoy sex with your mistress?' she asked excitedly, much to Sahria's amusement.

'I – I enjoy it with either sex,' Aisha admitted, blushing shamefully. 'I always have.'

Calema smiled and smoothed gloved hand over the girl's lithe form until she cupped her down-covered pussy, and Aisha shuddered with pleasure and closed her eyes.

'Calema, leave her,' said Sahria, and her friend reluctantly moved away from the girl and sat back on the couch, a petulant expression on her face. 'So, if you were having sex with both your master and your mistress, why did she become jealous?'

'Each week the master would invite some of his male friends to join us. They would make love to both his wife and to me, but it soon became obvious that they all preferred me.'

'Then you must have had sex with a great number of men.'

Aisha nodded. 'I love it, mistress,' she said in a voice that rang with inappropriate innocence.

'You will be a favourite of the prince, of that I am sure.'

'I hope so, mistress,' replied Aisha, and then her expression suddenly took on a look of concern. 'There will be others, won't there, mistress? It won't just be the prince?'

Sahria laughed and ran her fingers through the lustrous tresses of the girl's hair. 'Don't worry, my sweet little nymphet. There will be many a fine prick straining to satisfy your hunger. But first, like the others, you must learn subservience.' She crouched down and gazed at Aisha's pouting sex lips, finding it hard to imagine that such a dainty hole could accommodate the thick erection of a rampant male. Aisha moved her hips forward in invitation, as if expecting similar treatment to that which Zia had enjoyed with Calema. Sahria was tempted, but merely kissed the downy hair lightly, and then stood up. 'Step back in line,' she said, before moving to stand before the next in line.

She now faced a girl of apparently oriental descent. Sahria signalled with her whip and the girl removed her smock. Her breasts were full and her stomach flat, curving sensuously to her bushy groin. Her olive skin glowed in the sunlight. 'Your name?' she demanded, but the girl said nothing. 'What is your name?' repeated Sahria. 'Speak!'

The girl's narrow eyes widened in terror but she remained silent, so Sahria raised the whip and the girl cowered fearfully. 'I said speak!' Sahria roared.

'Mistress...' Aisha interrupted cautiously.

'Silence!' snapped Sahria, glaring at the girl. 'Speak your name or your punishment will be most severe!' But the girl shook her head. Furious, Sahria brought the whip down and lashed her across her buttocks. She gasped with pain but still said nothing.

'Mistress, please,' said Aisha, her voice trembling, 'she cannot.'

Sahria lowered the whip. 'What do you mean?'

Aisha rested her hand on the sobbing girl's shoulder. 'Mistress, she can hear what you say, but she cannot speak. She is mute.'

Sahria stepped back guiltily. The girl whimpered quietly as tears ran down her lovely face. Sahria felt she should apologise, but then considered that to do so might be taken as a sign of weakness. After a few awkward moments she moved forward, cupped the girl's face, and kissed her passionately, full on the mouth. The girl stiffened with shock, but quickly relaxed and responded by parting her lips slightly to allow Sahria's tongue to slip between them. The embrace lasted a good few moments, and then Sahria stepped back, and the girl smiled.

'Does anyone here know her name?' she asked of the group, but they shook their heads. She looked into the girl's eyes, still wet with tears. 'Can you write your name?' she said softly. The girl nodded, so Calema searched and found a crayon and some parchment, which she handed to Sahria. She gave them to the girl and she wrote quickly with trembling hands, and then gave the paper back.

'Su-Lee,' said Sahria, 'a lovely name.' The girl smiled and motioned that she wished to write something else. Sahria handed the parchment back and she scrawled a few words before shyly holding the paper out in front of her. Sahria read the words with astonishment. Under her name, Su-Lee had written, *Beat me again*, in clear but shaky handwriting.

Sahria shook her head. 'I cannot,' she said, 'you have not done anything to deserve further punishment.'

Su-Lee's response was to turn and bend with her ankles together, her legs straight and her hands resting on the floor. Sahria looked at her upturned bottom, marked by a single red welt, and her mind raced. This was an open act of defiance that must not go unpunished, but the girl actually wanted to be lashed, and the other girls stood in silent expectation.

'You will not be beaten simply because you wish it,' Sahria decreed at last. '*I* will decide when the lash is to be used. You will not demand it of me.' She heard Su-Lee sigh with disappointment as she began to rise, and for some reason this infuriated her, so without warning she whipped her with incredible force across her bottom. Every girl in the group gasped with shock and Su-Lee fell forward onto her hands and knees.

Sahria smiled cruelly. 'As I said, *I* will decide.' She looked at Calema, who nodded in approval.

The next girl stepped forward and removed her smock without being asked to do so. She had similar colouring and features to Zia, but was shorter in height.

'I am called Jo-Jo,' she said proudly.

'Did I ask you to speak?' said Sahria, with mock anger, and the girl looked crestfallen as Sahria turned to her friend. 'Calema, thrash this one for her impertinence.'

Calema bowed and took the whip from Sahria.

'Turn and bend forward,' Sahria commanded Jo-Jo. The frightened girl immediately did as ordered, and Sahria admired the globes of her buttocks as Calema prepared to administer the punishment. Then Sahria turned to face the remainder of the group of girls.

'Know this, my pretty waifs,' she began. 'You will not speak unless ordered, and you will obey instructions without question. Otherwise, you will feel the kiss of the lash, or,' she looked at Su-Lee, 'something more appropriate.

'Now, administer the punishment,' she said vehemently.

Calema raised her arm high and brought the whip down fiercely onto the girl's plump bottom. Her buttocks quivered and she yelped. A second stroke cut her across her bottom, then a third and a fourth. The welts appeared quickly. Calema had certainly developed considerable expertise in the art of flagellation.

'Enough,' Sahria ordered, and Calema immediately handed her the whip and resumed her place on the couch. The sobbing girl remained in her bent position. She had learned her lesson well.

'Stand,' Sahria said, and the girl obeyed, her tearful eyes shining with excitement, and the lush hairs between her legs glistening with obvious dampness. 'Now, Jo-Jo,' said Sahria in a gentler tone, 'tell us about yourself.'

Jo-Jo took a deep breath, and then began. 'I am seventeen and I have had sex with seventeen men,' she said proudly, although her voice was trembling slightly.

'Have you ever had sex with a woman?' asked Calema.

'No. In that respect I am still a virgin.'

'You will not be before this day is out,' teased Calema.

'When are we going to meet some men?' asked Aisha excitedly, attracting a glare from Sahria. 'Sorry, mistress,' the blonde added hastily, realising her sin and bowing fearfully.

Sahria chose to ignore her outburst and moved to stand before the last two girls. They were as alike as jewels in a royal crown, and of Persian descent. 'Ah,' she said, 'twin sisters. The prince will like that, I am sure. Remove your clothing so we may see if you are alike in every way.'

The two girls did as ordered until they stood as naked as the others. They were trim and shapely, and Sahria noticed immediately that they both had their nipples pierced with small gold rings. 'What are your names?'

she asked.

'I am Shalma, and this is my sister, Lisha,' said one. The two girls bowed reverently as she spoke.

'Go on.'

'We are nineteen years of age.' It was the second girl who spoke this time. 'We were sold into sex slavery by our uncle following the death of our parents, two years ago. We have served many masters.'

'Did your masters beat you?'

'Invariably,' replied Shalma, 'and never without cause.'

'Do you take pleasure in pain?'

'Always,' said Lisha, with an easy smile, 'and we like to share our experiences together.'

'You must have learnt much from your experiences,' said Calema.

'There is always more that can be discovered.'

'Quite so,' said Sahria. 'What would you say if I told you that I was going to beat you now?'

The girls looked shocked. 'We have not given you cause to punish us,' protested Lisha. 'Surely it would not be right.'

'I agree,' said her sister, 'we have obeyed your every command. You cannot punish us.'

'The very fact that you have the temerity to voice your objections is reason enough,' Sahria pointed out. 'Am I not your mistress?'

The two girls bowed their heads in acknowledgement of Sahria's words. 'Turn and stand together,' she continued. 'After all, you did say that you enjoy sharing your experiences, did you not?'

Shalma and Lisha said nothing, but turned and stood

meekly to await their punishment.

'Press close together,' ordered Sahria, and the sisters moved closer so that their hips touched. 'You will receive just one cut, as a warning to you all that we demand total obedience.'

She raised her arm and waited. The twins stood erect, their heads held proudly, and Sahria purposely let them wait. The other girls watched in silence, scarcely daring to breathe. The two Persians hardly moved, standing without the slightest sign of trembling, clearly well used to chastisement.

Sahria aimed carefully. Bringing the whip down swiftly she ensured the lash cut across both bottoms with equal ferocity. There was no sound from either girl – not even the slightest whimper. She was tempted to administer more strokes, but knew that she must keep her word. Once must suffice.

She threw the flail down onto a table and perched on a high stool. 'You may turn and face me,' she said. The twins obeyed and stood together without a trace of emotion showing on their faces. Sahria looked at the line of girls. They were each beautiful in their own way. The prince would be pleased.

But first they had to be trained and corrected. They had strong personalities and had to be taught total subservience. It would not be an easy task. Shalma and Lisha would probably be the most difficult to train; they had no doubt experienced much during their time of slavery and had become hardened to pain. She gestured to them. 'Come and kneel before me,' she commanded.

She arched her back and pushed her hips forward,

while spreading her legs wide. The two girls stared at the proffered sight of her wet sex lips. 'Lick me,' she said, 'both of you at the same time.' Shalma and Lisha looked at each other. 'I said lick me. Refuse and I will see to it that your bottoms are cut to ribbons.'

The girls leaned in, gingerly moving their mouths closer and closer to Sahria's pussy. Lisha pushed out her tongue and the tip touched Sahria's outer lips, and then drew her tongue back immediately. Then Shalma did the same, and it was clear that neither girl had tasted the scent of a woman before.

'Lick me,' repeated Sahria. 'Do it like you would have a man do it to you. You know what pleases a woman – make me come in your mouths or it will be bad for you, I promise!'

The twins began to lap around her moist opening. Slowly they warmed to the task and started to suckle and nibble her outer lips whilst delving their tongues into her and alternately licking across her hard bud. Sahria sensed a great feeling of power and dominance as she watched the two proud girls serve her. They would obey her without question in future.

'Enough,' she said presently. She hadn't come, but this time it was not necessary. The lesson had been learned, and the twins moved from her and rejoined the line.

Sahria stood up and faced the group. 'We will break for one hour, to give you all time to reflect upon what you have witnessed. I want you to go to the blue chambers. There you will find many exotic items of clothing. You will each select that which you feel suits you best and dress accordingly, then return here.

Following this the lessons will begin in earnest.

'Some of you are sexually experienced and some are not. You will be taught subservience to men, and you will be instructed in ways in which to please your lovers so that they never forget you. As one of the twins wisely said, there is always much that can be learned.'

Chapter Eight

Sahria and Calema were sitting on opposite sofas sipping cool glasses of wine. The room was becoming hot as the sun rose higher, and the atmosphere was stifling. Calema had removed her rubber hood and was teasing her blonde hair through her fingers.

Two Nubian menservants stood impassively, cooling the girls with large fans made from ostrich feathers. Sahria regarded them with a wry smile. These were the same two men who had turned on her, and now they were once more at her beck and call, by orders of the prince.

She allowed her eyes to feast on their muscular bodies and remembered how they had taken her. At first she had been unwilling; it was unheard of for a princess to consort with a slave. Even soldiers were supposed to be forbidden, although neither she nor Calema paid much heed to that particular ruling. Most of the palace garrison had succumbed to one or both of them at some time or other.

Sahria had struggled with the Nubians, and scratched and gouged their flesh with her fingernails, but when they removed their loincloths and revealed their magnificent manhoods she relaxed at once and offered herself to them.

She began to think of how they had used and abused her. It was wonderfully satisfying, the sort of sexual experience she'd been missing. It had always been *her* who had taken the lead and issued the orders, but then she found herself at the mercy of these two burly hulks.

They fucked her in turn and then, incredibly, they both fed their erections into her cunt simultaneously, stretching her flesh to the limit. Her pussy throbbed as she remembered the delightful pain as the two men thrust in and out of her and how, despite her fear and anger at the time, she had come over and over again.

'The girls will be returning soon,' said Calema, breaking Sahria's train of thought. 'What do you think of them?'

'They are all very lovely. I am sure the prince will be very pleased.'

'Are you jealous?'

'No, of course not.' Sahria stroked between her legs nonchalantly. 'Once I had savoured the prince's wonderful cock, all such thoughts were dismissed from my mind. Now it is my pleasure to serve him in any way he chooses.'

Calema looked incredulously at her friend. It was clear that she didn't believe a word.

The door to the chamber opened slowly, and Calema and Sahria looked up expectantly. Instead of the return of their pupils, however, two other girls entered. After a moment Sahria recognised them as the same two the prince had taken to his bedchamber. They looked weary and bedraggled and their short smocks were torn.

'Princess Sahria?' asked one, a delicately framed girl with short brown hair and a pale complexion.

'I am *Mistress* Sahria,' came the curt reply. 'And this is Mistress Calema.'

The girl bowed and slumped onto another sofa. Her companion, a taller girl with a shock of bright red hair joined her without a word.

'Did I say you could sit?' demanded Sahria angrily as she rose and towered over the two exhausted figures.

'Please, mistress,' said the second girl, 'we are drained. The prince is a most demanding lover.'

'Stand!' barked Sahria. Shocked at her sharp tone, the two girls quickly struggled to their feet. 'Remove your smocks!' They obeyed without another word while Sahria examined their bodies dispassionately. The smaller girl had tiny breasts and a lithe shape, with a small tuft of fluffy down between her legs.

The red-haired girl was opposite to her companion in every way. Although very attractive and vivacious, she was far more voluptuous, with large breasts and broad hips. Sahria looked with interest from one to the other. It was clear that the prince enjoyed variety in his sexual encounters.

'Turn,' she ordered. The girls obeyed and Calema gasped. Their bottoms and upper thighs were scored with dozens of welts from the cane. Sahria ran her fingertips over the tortured globes of the smaller girl, and felt the ridges in her soft flesh. 'Why have you been punished so?' she asked gently.

'The prince was dissatisfied with us. We tried to please him but neither of us are experienced in such matters.' The girl took a sharp intake of breath as she was touched on a particularly sensitive spot. Sahria stepped back.

'Turn to face me,' she said, her tone softening somewhat. 'What are your names?'

'I am Agita,' said the redhead.

'And I am Mena,' said the other.

'You say you are inexperienced?'

'I have had just one lover, other than the prince,' replied Agita.

'I am a virgin,' said Mena, as though ashamed of the fact.

'You mean you *were* a virgin,' laughed Calema.

'No, no, I still am,' Mena insisted. 'I think that is why the prince was so furious and beat us so severely. He is so large, he couldn't force it into me, it hurt me so much.'

'Don't worry, Mena,' said Sahria sympathetically, 'we will teach you the secrets that will enable you to accommodate any stalk that is offered. What else did the prince do to you, apart from giving you a thrashing?'

'After he had been inside Agita he tried me. When he couldn't he beat us both and then forced me to suck his weapon. I could taste Agita's scent.'

'Did you like it?' asked Calema. The girl hung her head and blushed noticeably.

'Come on,' insisted Sahria, 'don't be shy. There is no room for coyness here. Did you like the taste of your friend's pussy?'

'I... yes, mistress,' Mena said quietly.

'Would you like to lick Agita between the legs?'

The girl looked astonished by the suggestion. 'No! No, I couldn't!' she insisted.

Sahria smiled and pushed the girl's head down until

her face was close to Agita's groin. 'Go on,' she whispered. 'She'll taste delightful.'

Mena hesitated, and then knelt and moved even closer to Agita's sex. Sahria looked at the bigger girl and saw that a faint smile of excitement was playing across her lips. 'Go on,' Sahria repeated. 'Lick it…'

Mena moved cautiously and pushed her tongue out, the tip just appearing between her lips, then suddenly she pulled back, shaking her head. 'I can't, mistress,' she sobbed. 'I just can't!'

Sahria smiled and stroked the girl's face gently. 'You will, Mena. Before long you will taste the juices of many girls and you will grow to love it. Now, you were both very rude to me when you entered the room, so you must be punished.'

'Oh no, mistress,' protested Agita. 'No more, please. My bottom stings so.'

Sahria grinned cruelly and the two girls hung their heads. There was a long pause, and Mena began to tremble, clearly terrified.

'I will not beat you this time,' said Sahria. 'Your punishment will be humiliation. You will remain naked for one week, or until I say you may dress.'

'A week, mistress?' queried Mena, aghast.

'One week. Wherever you go in the palace or out to the town, you will appear naked. What say you to this?'

There was another pause, and then Agita raised her head. 'Thank you, mistress,' she said simply.

'And you, Mena?'

The girl looked directly into her eyes. 'I will obey, mistress, but if you wish to beat me as well I will not object.'

'Another time,' said Sahria, musing on how odd it was that Mena and Su-Lee, the two smallest girls of the group, took so much apparent pleasure in being whipped.

The door to the chamber opened again and the other girls returned. Each was dressed in some form of revealing garment, some made of leather, some of silk, but all erotic in the extreme. They had all chosen well.

'Two of you here have admitted to being virgins,' Sahria said. 'Before the real lessons begin we must deal with the matter.' She looked at Zia, who returned her glance with a smile. 'Come forward, Zia. The rest of you may sit.'

The tall Nubian stepped forward to face her. She was dressed in a tight white leather basque, which accentuated her voluptuous form and emphasised her deep ebony colouring. She stood proudly before the others while Sahria turned to Calema.

'Go and fetch one of the soldiers,' she said matter-of-factly, and Calema left the room immediately.

Sahria looked at the two black servants who were busily fanning the assembled group. One or both of them would do for Mena, she decided, but Zia must be treated differently. After all, she was a princess.

Presently Calema returned, accompanied by a bemused looking guard. He was dressed simply in a regulation skirt and studded leather jerkin, and was still clutching his spear. Sahria took the weapon from him and laid it against a wall, and he looked around at the group of lovely females, his eyes wide.

'Now, brave soldier, this is Zia,' Sahria told him.

The guard leered at Zia's mouth-watering breasts as

she moved towards him, and Sahria saw to her satisfaction, that the front of his skirt was already starting to rise. 'Zia is a virgin,' she went on. 'She will respond to your every whim and obey any command. All we ask is that you take her with respect.'

The soldier looked at her incredulously. 'You mean, you want me to... to have sex with her?'

'Of course,' Sahria replied, in disbelief that he should ask such a stupid question. The soldier glanced around the room again, evidently concerned that this was some sort of a trick, then he grinned and took hold of Zia's arm. He made to escort her from the room, but Sahria stopped him. 'No, no, you must do it here, now,' she said.

The guard looked around at the other girls again. 'You mean, in front of everybody?' he asked fearfully.

'Can you not do that?' Sahria goaded. 'Are you ashamed to show us all what hangs between your legs?'

He glanced around again and then looked back at Zia, staring once more at her irresistible breasts. 'No, I'm not,' he gasped suddenly, 'and yes, I can do it!'

Sahria smiled wryly and sat down on a couch next to Calema.

The beautiful Nubian and the anxious soldier stood motionless for some moments. Eventually Zia looked directly at him and spoke impatiently. 'What would you have me do?' she asked.

The guard reached out and nervously cupped Zia's breasts in his rough hands. She smiled, reached under his skirt, withdrew his stiff cock, and rubbed him with clear expertise.

'Are you sure you are a virgin?' asked Sahria, and Zia looked at her, her deep brown eyes shining with lust.

'I have done this many times,' she said quietly as she continued to masturbate the trembling soldier. 'And this...' She crouched in front of him and took his cock into her mouth, enveloping the erection with her sensual lips. The guard groaned and Sahria feared he might come before the deed was done. Zia, too, must have realised the danger, for she pulled away quickly and stopped rubbing him.

'Turn and present yourself,' ordered Sahria, 'before he loses control.' Zia obeyed at once. She turned her back to the soldier and bent forward until her hands touched the floor, her legs held straight and spread slightly apart. Sahria gazed appreciatively at the sumptuous curves of her perfect bottom, the deep cleft between her buttocks and the engorged lips of her glistening cunt. The guard shuffled forward, his cock jutting like a spear, ready to impale his victim. The other girls crowded closer to witness their companion's defloration. Sahria smiled to herself; Zia would be a more than responsive pupil, of that she was certain.

The guard gripped Zia's bottom and thrust his bursting cock deep into her virgin hole in one swift movement. Zia moaned, but it was a cry of pleasure, not discomfort. He began to pump in and out of her luscious body, and it was obvious that he wouldn't last long. Suddenly he pulled from her, and she turned immediately and knelt before him, taking hold of his cock and rubbing it frantically. The first jet of his creamy release arced across her face and then she took the bulbous head into her mouth and suckled him, swallowing heavily until he had no more to give.

When he was done, Zia released him from the heavenly grip of her lips and stood erect. 'That was too quick,' she said simply to Sahria, who studied her eyes. The tall African was goading her. Her expression was once more proud and defiant. Sahria realised she had made it too easy for her; the mere fact of being fucked in front of the others had had no effect on her. Sahria decided that the girl would be severely punished for her pride and disdain.

'Rejoin the others,' she said quietly, and turned to look at Mena. 'Come forward,' she commanded, and Mena rose sheepishly and walked slowly towards her. Her impish frame was trembling and her face was ashen. Sahria sensed a warm glow of satisfaction at the girl's anguish. 'How old are you, Mena?' she asked.

'Seventeen, mistress.'

'You look younger. Are you sure you are seventeen?'

Mena looked up at her. 'Yes, mistress, I swear it.'

Sahria shrugged; it was of no great importance.

'Are you ready to be deflowered?' she asked, and Mena suddenly broke into tears.

'Oh please, mistress,' she sobbed, 'I am so afraid. When the prince tried to enter me it hurt so much.'

Sahria rested a hand on the quaking girl's shoulder. 'That is because you were not adequately prepared,' she said. 'I will see to it that the tiny treasure between your legs becomes so oiled with your juices that you will barely notice the thrusting of the man's weapon. But first, perhaps a few strokes of the cane will warm your body and help you relax.'

Mena looked up at her through tearful eyes, her expression transformed into one of delight. Sahria nodded towards Calema, who produced a thin cane and handed it to her. Mena eyed the switch and ran her tongue across her upper lip. Sahria began to wonder how she would ever be able to adequately punish the girl, should she be given cause.

'Lie across the sofa,' she suddenly ordered, and Mena obeyed at once, happily moving to a nearby couch and spreading herself along it on her stomach. Sahria took a large cushion and forced it under the girl's hips so that her bottom arched provocatively, the porcelain skin of her buttocks already scored with the marks of her previous chastisement.

Sahria raised the cane and paused. Mena glanced over her shoulder and looked fearfully at the switch, and then buried her face in the cushions. Sahria noticed she had stiffened her buttocks. 'Relax, Mena,' she ordered quietly. The girl's globes softened and Sahria swept the cane down, cutting her squarely across her bottom. Mena yelped, the sound of her protest lost in the envelope of the cushions. Sahria whipped her again with a little more force. This time the girl made no sound. Instead she arched her back in readiness for more punishment, clearly enjoying what must have been excruciating pain.

Sahria administered the third blow with all the force she could muster. Mena yelped again, and Sahria dropped the cane to the floor and proudly examined the three new stripes that were quickly forming across the girl's tortured bottom. She had scored her deeply;

the marks would remain for some days to come.

'Turn over onto your back,' she said after a few moments, and Mena obeyed, lying in naked innocence, her gaze fixed on Sahria. The cheeks of her face were flushed and her eyes shone with excitement. Sahria turned to Calema. 'Prepare her,' she said.

Calema sat on the edge of the couch, stroked Mena's legs, and gently parted them. Her tiny pussy looked too small to accommodate even a finger, and Sahria felt no surprise that she had experienced such difficulty in absorbing the prince's mighty length.

Calema moved forward and rested her head on Mena's slim thighs. Her face was inches away from the downy covered lips between her legs. She blew gently on the sparse curls, then licked the tops of her thighs, purposely avoiding the touch of her tongue to the dampening hole. Mena whimpered softly and moved her hips as though attempting to persuade Calema to put her mouth to her virgin prize, but Calema continued to tease her. Mena stroked Calema's blonde hair, and then suddenly gripped it tightly, tugging her face against her pussy.

Sahria could hear the wet sounds as her friend began to devour the girl's sex, and then watched avidly as Calema moved back slightly so that Sahria was able to see the tip of her tongue flicking rapidly against the girl's bud.

Mena gasped and began to moan louder, raising her legs and drawing her thighs back against her breasts. Sahria glanced at the two Nubian servants. They were both dutifully fanning the writhing couple, but their loincloths bulged with their erections. One of them was looking with more than a little interest at Calema's bottom, which was sensuously exposed through the rubber suit that encased her lovely body.

Suddenly Mena squealed in orgasm, and Calema lapped her pussy until her cries of delight subsided. When she was clearly certain that the girl was completely sated she sat back and gently stirred her fingers inside Mena's oily sex. She looked at Sahria and smiled, her face coated with the girl's juices. 'She is ready,' she breathed.

Mena sat up suddenly, the look of anguish returning to her flushed face. 'No…' she cried, 'I am afraid. It will hurt…'

Sahria sighed in exasperation. 'Shalma, Lisha, take her arms,' she ordered. The twins did as commanded, clutching Mena's wrists tightly. 'Zia and Agita, take her ankles and spread her legs wide.'

Mena tried to struggle, but the two girls grasped her legs and held them firmly on either side of the low couch. Sahria moved to one of the male servants, took his fan from him, and dropped it to the floor. Looking meaningfully into his eyes, she unclasped his loincloth and the flimsy material fell from his body, leaving him naked, his stalk jutting aggressively. She gripped the bone-hard flesh and tugged it, dragging him towards the squirming girl. She stood next to the servant, still holding his black cock.

'Don't you want this, Mena?' she teased. 'Surely you cannot resist such a prize.'

'I *do* want it,' the girl whimpered, 'but it is so big. I am afraid…' Her words trailed into a whisper as Sahria released her grip and the man knelt between her legs, and she stared wide-eyed at the jutting monster that rose like a serpent from his bushy groin. He gripped his cock by the root, aiming the head at her succulence. Sahria could see the girl was ready; there would be little or no pain.

The servant pressed the bulbous end of his stalk against her sex lips and then pushed. The gnarled rod sank into her slowly, he paused when she had accepted about half his length, and then pushed again until their groins met.

'*Ohhh…*' was all Mena could utter, as he began to fuck her with long slow strokes, gripping her narrow hips with his huge hands. She moaned softly and closed her eyes. The girls released their grip of her wrists and ankles and she wrapped her arms and legs around his heavy body. She dug her heels into his thrusting buttocks and clawed at his back.

Sahria nodded towards the other servant, who immediately dropped his fan and tore off his loincloth, his cock spearing from his hairy groin. He strode over to the rutting couple and held his stiffness close to Mena's face. She must have sensed his presence because she opened her eyes and stared at the proffered monster, then grasped it in her hand. Her fingers could barely circle the thick stalk, but she rubbed him inexpertly as he pushed it closer to her face. It was clear what he wanted, but Mena seemed reluctant at first, and merely kissed the tip lightly. The other servant was pumping into her hard and fast, swamping her with his bulk. Her lips peeled open in a silent scream and the other demanding cock sank into her mouth. She was unable to accommodate much of his length.

Her cheeks bulged as he tried to press more into her, and then he withdrew slightly to allow her to lick around his bulbous knob. Sahria smiled with satisfaction as she watched this erstwhile virgin pleasure two men simultaneously.

Suddenly the man who was fucking her pulled away and shuffled across her supine form to present his weapon to her face. She let the cock slip from between her lips and the first man immediately came, sending jet after jet of thick cream into her open mouth. Barely had he finished when the other servant followed suit, coating her face with his copious juices. Mena squealed with joy as her own orgasm tore through her young body and the other girls clapped and cheered with delight. She writhed and bucked her hips, almost forcing the man squatting over her to fall from the couch, and she grabbed herself between the legs and rubbed frantically until she was drained.

The cheering stopped and the two men struggled to their feet. They donned their flimsy garments and once more took up the fans. Mena lay limp, allowing the movements of the fans to cool her sweating body. Her face and hair were coated with streaks of jism and her expression was one of total satisfaction.

'Do you feel ready for the prince, Mena?' Sahria asked.

'Oh yes, mistress,' she panted. 'I feel ready for anything.'

'There is a lesson to be learnt here,' continued Sahria, addressing the entire group. 'Anything is possible, and indeed most pleasurable, with the right preparation. You will learn much from Mistress

Calema and myself and I am sure from each other. By the time we have finished with you the prince will want no other consorts.'

Hearing this, the girls giggled and chattered excitedly.

'Silence!' barked Sahria. 'You may not laugh without permission. Now you must all be punished.'

The room fell into silence.

'A dormitory has been set aside for you to the rear of these chambers. Go there now, remove all clothing, select a bed each, and await my displeasure.'

The girls trooped out of the room sullenly and headed in the direction she had indicated.

'What are you going to do with them?' asked Calema.

'The prince will visit us shortly. I want him to see that we have subjugated them all.'

'And how will you do that?'

'Just you wait and see,' Sahria said, with a knowing smile.

Sahria strode purposefully through the door to the dormitory, followed by Calema, who was carrying numerous short lengths of rope. The girls were all sitting dutifully and in silence, one to each of the rude metal cots. The room was sparsely furnished and meanly decorated. There were no curtains to draw across the large windows and the sun streamed in, the atmosphere stifling.

'You will kneel on your beds, facing the wall with your bottoms held high,' Sahria instructed. 'Be proud of your little backsides, ladies, they are your most prized assets.' The girls glanced at each other in apparent confusion, and Sahria clapped her hands angrily. 'Quickly!' she demanded, and they rushed to obey.

Soon they were all kneeling with their bottoms presented to her gaze. Before her were eight perfect posteriors, some scored with the marks of the lash or cane, others smooth, all inviting. Their shapes ranged from the boyish charm of Mena's little bum, to Agita's fleshy mounds.

Sahria took some of the ropes from Calema and motioned to her friend to begin at the end of the line, while she moved to Zia, who occupied the narrow cot nearest the door. Sahria gazed hungrily at her superb sable buttocks. Their arrogant thrust seemed to be demanding immediate satisfaction, and Sahria vowed that it wouldn't be long before she was able to witness the thickest of cocks plundering the virginal depths of Zia's sweet arse.

Three dark red stripes decorated the otherwise flawless globes, enticingly criss-crossing each other. Sahria parted Zia's buttocks and admired her dark anus. She licked her lips but resisted the temptation to run her tongue in the deep cleft. There was work to be done.

Deftly she tied lengths of rope around Zia's wrists and ankles, and then secured them to the corners of the metal cot. Moving to the next she repeated the operation with Aisha. As she looked at her sweetly upturned bottom Sahria wondered how the girl could be so promiscuous and yet manage to appear so innocent. She ran her fingertips along Aisha's silky pussy lips from behind, and imagined a succession of demanding cocks slipping effortlessly between them; another vision she fully intended to enjoy for real in the none too distant future!

Next it was the turn of Su-Lee, the beautiful mute oriental. Once she had fully restrained her Sahria slapped the girl's bruised bottom with the palm of her hand. Su-Lee gasped with delight, so Sahria slapped her again, and then moved on.

Now it was the turn of Jo-Jo, the curvaceous Nubian. Although she was positioned in exactly the same manner as all the others, her bottom appeared even more inviting to Sahria. The sensuous globes of dark flesh glistened with perspiration, and the pert thrust of her buttocks was such that her anus and the fleshy folds of her sex lips were clearly visible.

Sahria tied her firmly to the bed and then knelt between her legs. It was too much for her to resist, so she bent forward and licked the sweat from the deep valley between Jo-Jo's buttocks. Her taste was sweet and her scent was arousing in the extreme. Sahria circled the black sphincter with her tongue and then prodded inside. Jo-Jo moaned with pleasure.

Sahria raised herself and slapped the girl's bottom, and then moved to stand once more in the centre of the room. Calema joined her, having securely bound the other four girls to their beds. Sahria surveyed the scene before her; eight wonderfully feminine bottoms, ready for the prince's pleasure. She felt justifiably proud; Sarne would surely be delighted with her work.

Sahria returned with Calema to the main chamber, leaving the girls to wonder as to their fate. She beckoned to one of the servants. 'Go to the prince and ask him to attend us,' she ordered. The servant bowed low and then left to deliver her request.

'Do you think Prince Sarne will be pleased?' Calema asked uncertainly.

'He will be delighted,' Sahria answered confidently. 'How could it be any other way? The girls are beautiful and totally servile. They are more than ready to do his bidding, every one of them. Even Mena has been prepared in order to accommodate his weapon without too much pain. Yes, the prince will be pleased.'

The door opened and two burly guards entered the room. They stood motionless on either side of the door as Prince Sarne walked in. He was dressed simply, wearing just a leather skirt and tunic.

'They are prepared for me already?' he asked incredulously, and Sahria nodded. 'Then take me to them,' he demanded.

The two females led the way, closely followed by the prince and his guards. They entered the dormitory and the door was closed behind them. Sahria and Calema stood back proudly, while Sarne stood in silence for some moments, and then walked slowly along the line of beds looking carefully at each upturned pair of buttocks.

He swung around suddenly to face Sahria and Calema. 'Why are they not all marked?' he demanded.

'It was not always necessary,' replied Sahria, more than a little confused by his apparent anger.

'Of course it is necessary!' he exploded. 'All women must know the pleasures of pain and servitude before they can fully understand the delights of submission and true subservience! Fetch me a switch! I will thrash them all!'

Calema scurried out of the room to search for a cane. 'I don't understand, my lord,' protested Sahria. 'They are all willing. Even Mena, the virgin you could not deflower, has been prepared and will now easily accept your wondrous penis.'

The prince walked along the line of cots again until he came to Mena. He stroked her soft bottom and then slipped his fingers into the succulence of her pussy. 'She is indeed well oiled,' he said, 'and her backside has been severely beaten.' He put his wet fingertips to his lips and Sahria saw to her relief that the front of his skirt was rising. Perhaps she would be forgiven.

Sarne licked Mena's juices from his fingers and then slapped her bottom, causing her to cry out. He walked back to stand facing Sahria and stared unblinkingly into her eyes. 'My orders were explicit,' he said calmly. 'They were to be fully prepared. You have chosen to ignore my instructions.'

'Please, my lord, I—'

'Silence! You will be severely punished. But first, I will do your work for you.'

Calema returned as he spoke, and he snatched the cane from her and marched quickly to stand beside Zia's cot. He raised the switch and then brought it down swiftly across her rump. Zia cried out in pain, but Sarne ignored her and moved to stand next to Aisha.

'See?' he bellowed. 'Not a mark! Not even a bruise from a slap! Her arse should be red-raw by now. How will this girl ever know true pleasure if she has never experienced real pain?' He brought the cane down on Aisha's pert bottom and she yelped. He administered four more hard cuts on her and then moved to Su-Lee. A single stroke across her already welted buttocks seemed to satisfy him, because he moved on immediately to stand beside Jo-Jo.

'Such a fine, arse,' he muttered, his expression breaking into a leer. 'How could you resist such an invitation?'

Sahria lost count of the number of times the cane whipped across the poor girl's bottom before he moved to Shalma and then to Lisha, dealing with them in similar fashion. For some reason he ignored Mena and moved to the last bed. Agita knelt before him, her bottom already heavily scored from the beating he had previously administered. A single but nevertheless painful stroke was all she suffered.

The prince dropped the cane and then stood behind Mena's bed. He stared at her severely marked buttocks. 'Beautiful,' he was heard to mutter under his breath. He pulled his skirt back to reveal the full extent of his erection and clambered onto the mattress behind the trembling girl.

Sahria noticed Mena grip the ropes that secured her wrists to the bed, and knew she was terrified.

'Let us see just how well you have prepared this one,' Sarne hissed. He gripped his cock by the root and pushed the bulbous tip against her puffy sex lips. Suddenly he lunged forward and plunged in to the hilt. Mena whimpered pitifully, but he merely laughed. He withdrew until she held just the head of his weapon inside her body, and then thrust forward again until his belly slapped against her bottom. Mena cried out once more, but this time Sahria knew it was a cry of delight.

Sarne pulled from her and clambered from the bed. He pulled his skirt across himself to conceal his already wilting phallus. Sahria wondered at his self-control, and glanced at Mena. She could see her juices trickling down the insides of her thighs, and knew that her young charge had enjoyed the experience immensely. She also considered that Sarne could at least not fail to be pleased with this part of the preparation.

The prince turned to his guards. 'Take Mistress Sahria and Mistress Calema to the black chambers,' he said. 'Strip them, fuck them, and then have Rapite prepare them for the snake!'

Chapter Nine

Sahria struggled valiantly but in vain as the soldiers shackled her once more to the rigid wooden frame in Rapite's dismal dungeon. This was all so unfair, she felt. She and Calema had done all that he had asked of them; the pupils could not have been more submissive. Prince Sarne could have done anything that took his fancy, the girls were bound and shackled as he would have expected, their bottoms presented for penetration or punishment. He could have had all eight of them; they would have complied without a murmur.

The final buckle was snapped into place and she was once again standing, naked and vulnerable, facing the rough unyielding surface of the frame. She looked over her shoulder at Calema. Her friend was lying on her stomach over a low bench with her wrists and ankles tied by thick ropes. Two large cushions had been placed under her groin to force her bottom up in an obscene display of submissive availability.

Calema looked up at her and smiled, her eyes filled with an abject declaration of lust. There was no anger or shame in her expression. She was clearly enjoying her predicament. Sahria felt a familiar twinge between her legs and had to admit to herself that she too was becoming rapidly aroused. She pictured the sight of the prince whipping the girls on their cots with the vicious switch, and tried to imagine what it had been like for them – and the thought thrilled her.

One of the guards approached Calema from behind and raised his skirt. His cock jutted from his groin, proud and erect. He crouched over the bench and aimed his tool at his lush target. Sahria saw Calema's eyes widen as he slipped his length inside her in one, easy push. She turned her face away, feeling both envious and strangely embarrassed in the witnessing of her friend's pleasure.

She felt a rough pair of hands pawing her buttocks and knew it would soon be her turn. Although the juices were running from her engorged sex lips she was nevertheless becoming increasingly furious. 'Get your filthy hands off me, soldier!' she hissed.

But the man merely laughed and slapped her bottom. She tugged at her bonds and writhed angrily. She knew it was useless, but found that she was experiencing an incongruous delight in her struggle. The guard slapped her backside again.

'Be still, princess,' he growled. 'I have something nice for you.' She felt him dig his thumb between her buttocks and his fingers slid into the warm wetness of her pussy. 'The bitch is soaked,' he sneered to his rutting companion.

'So is this one,' panted the other. 'I swear you could get in here with me!' They both laughed, the fingers were removed from between Sahria's sex, and then she felt the familiar prodding of the head of a very hard cock against her moist opening. The soldier slid his length into her with the utmost ease.

'Oh, this is a hot one!' the man grunted as he began to pump steadily. He gripped her waist and dug his fingernails into her flesh. There was no finesse in his movements and no subtlety. Sahria was not surprised, she knew these ignorant animals were unlikely to know of the more delicate refinements of good sex. He was fucking her, as simple as that.

'I think I'll take this one in the arse,' panted his colleague.

'No…' Calema protested, with little conviction in her voice. Sahria glanced over her shoulder again and watched as her friend's lover forced his length into her bottom, and the joy on the girl's face was clear to see.

'Oh yes, she likes this,' her man breathed. Sahria's lover seemed content to thrust in and out of her, the frame creaking as he hammered against her body. Her breasts rubbed painfully against the rough wood and her nipples hardened. Suddenly, he grunted and she felt him throbbing within the tightness of her slippery sheath. She squeezed her thigh muscles, not to heighten his pleasure, but to attempt to force her own orgasm.

Then he was gone.

Sahria felt cheated, especially as she could hear her friend moaning with the joy of her release. The soldier stood by Sahria's side and looked directly into her face. She looked down contemptuously at his drooping phallus and then glanced back at him with a haughty expression. He covered himself with his skirt and she turned her head away. The soldier slapped her hard on the behind and then laughed loudly, to conceal his awkwardness.

The door opened noisily and the grisly form of Rapite

entered. 'What is this?' he demanded angrily. 'How dare you use my chambers in this way?'

'Master Rapite,' responded one of the guards quickly. 'We were ordered by the prince to bring these females to you.'

The squat man shuffled over to Sahria and put a hand against her moist sex. 'Were you also ordered to fuck them?' he said with a leer, as he put his wet fingers to his mouth and licked them.

'Er, yes sir, we were,' blurted the soldier.

Rapite laughed. 'Yes,' he said wryly, 'I expect you were.'

'You are to prepare them for the snake, my lord,' said the second soldier, and Rapite's beady eyes widened.

'The snake?' he said with some surprise. 'You must have been very wicked girls indeed!'

'What is this snake?' Sahria asked nervously.

'The word is not "what", it is "who",' chuckled Rapite. 'The snake is one who is in possession of such attributes that even you will be shocked, dear princess.'

Sahria swallowed hard. Surely this man – the one they called the snake – could not been endowed more than the prince himself! And, knowing Sarne's arrogance and pride, surely he would not permit such a man to exist in his kingdom? It then occurred to her that the man's weapon might be so grotesquely large as to be comical, more a source of amusement than envy, except of course to the hapless women who must accommodate the thing.

'You must be well prepared,' said Rapite, with an evil grin, then turned to the soldiers. 'Go and fetch four jugs of oil,' he barked, 'and then alert the snake that I have need of his services. Bid him attend me as soon as he is able.' Sahria swallowed hard again. *Four* jugs of oil? Just how big was this man?

The oil was brought quickly. Rapite ordered the men to set two of the jugs by the side of Calema, and then to place the remainder at Sahria's feet. The soldiers obeyed and then stood to attention as if awaiting further instructions. 'Go,' snapped Rapite. 'Leave us.'

'Sir?'

'I said go! I have no further need of you.'

Sahria watched them leave, the disappointment clear in their eyes.

When the heavy door was closed Rapite turned to look at her. 'I will thrash you both first,' he sneered. 'The snake likes to see a punished bottom.'

Sahria turned to face the wall, heard Rapite move across the room, and then she sensed him return to stand beside her. She looked round at him again. He was clutching the flat, forked tawse. Her pussy twitched; of all the implements that had been used to lash her poor bottom, this was the one she favoured the most.

She closed her eyes and waited excitedly for the pain, and it came quickly, a sharp blow to her right buttock followed by another to the other plump globe. The rough leather cut into her flesh, sending the pain searing throughout her tortured rear. At least ten more blows followed, each as vicious as the first, Rapite once more proving to be a master of his craft.

He moved to stand by the spread-eagled form of Calema, and Sahria watched hungrily as he administered a similar punishment. The tawse thwacked across the rosy-red cheeks of her friend's delightful bottom, over and over again, and Sahria noticed that not once did the joy leave Calema's face.

Rapite returned to Sahria and took up one of the jugs of oil. He cupped his free hand under her buttocks and then she felt the viscous liquid being poured down the cleft. He smoothed the oil into her pussy, then pushed his fingers and thumb effortlessly inside her. She breathed heavily, relaxing to his expert touch as he turned his hand within her delicate folds of flesh, and then spread his fingers to open her even more. She moaned softly. She sensed him make his hand into a fist and then he pushed deeper. Sahria groaned with pleasure; she had quickly come to enjoy this particular deviation.

He stooped to pick up the second jug of oil, his hand still deep within her clutching sheath. She felt the smooth liquid being poured over her bottom again, and then he moved his hand from inside her and eased two fingers into her anus. There was more oil and then more fingers until his hand was once more enveloped by her willing flesh, this time deep within her tight bottom.

Sahria had become happily used to such an unnatural intrusion, and found it easy to relax as Rapite probed her forbidden depths expertly, and she sighed with pleasure and thrust her buttocks invitingly. It was clear that, whatever physical attributes the snake possessed, she was going to have to accommodate him in both her oiled channels.

Rapite withdrew and shuffled over to Calema. From

her shackled position Sahria was unable to see fully what he was doing, but from the sounds of her friend's heavy moans it was apparent that Calema was now receiving similar treatment. Sahria tugged at her bonds, and the leather straps felt reassuringly tight.

Having completed his task, Rapite wiped his hands on a piece of linen, a broad grin across his twisted features. He ambled slowly to the door and opened it, then clapped his hands together twice. Sahria held her breath and watched as Rapite stepped back, and a tall hooded figure entered. He was covered entirely by a long black cape, with the hood drawn forward over his face and his hands tucked into the voluminous sleeves. She watched him move silently across the room. Turning her head, she saw him stand next to Calema, her perfect naked form stretched across the bench, totally at his mercy.

Unfolding his arms, he ran his hands over her pert, upturned bottom. He muttered something in an appreciative tone, and then moved to Sahria. He touched her bottom and lightly fondled each of the rounded globes, then slipped a finger deftly inside her anus. Despite the oil and Rapite's previous treatment of her, she managed to grip him tightly, tensing the ring of muscle around his probing finger.

'This one will be the first,' he breathed, as he eased his finger in and out of her like a small cock.

He withdrew and stood at her side. Suddenly, he threw back the hood of his cloak and revealed his grinning face. Sahria gasped. His skin was as black as ebony and was covered in tattoos. Images of beasts of the field and strange mythological creatures marked his features, as well as his bald head, each one of the tattoos beautifully crafted and richly coloured. As he moved the pictures seemed to come alive. He pulled back his cloak and stiffened his pectoral muscles, grinning as Sahria stared transfixed at the shifting images etched into his skin.

He threw off the cloak, allowing it to fall to the stone floor at his feet. Sahria at once saw that his entire body was similarly decorated, but it was not this that caused her to gasp again. Jutting from his shaven groin was not one but *two* hugely erect cocks, one above the other. Her first thought was that one of them must have been false, but as she looked wide-eyed at the proffered monsters she realised they were both genuine. Even singly they were larger than an average man's endowment, and together they presented an awesome sight.

Still grinning, the man moved behind her and gripped her upper thighs tightly. She felt the head of one of his stalks touch her pussy lips, and then the length slid effortlessly into her oiled sheath. She looked down the front of her body, could feel herself being expertly fucked, and yet she could see another stiff erection moving back and forth between her thighs, a sight she found strangely erotic.

The man moved back slightly and she felt him probing at her sex lips. Then he pushed slowly forward and she realised he was forcing both of his stiff rods into her stretched flesh. Sahria had taken two men in this way before on a number of occasions, but her past lovers had never possessed such wonderfully thick tools as those that were now plundering her. The pain was excruciatingly wonderful. He reached round and grasped her breasts, kneading the generous flesh. Each thrust of his hips sent a searing jab of pain shooting through her loins, causing her to cry out rhythmically. She came suddenly and violently with a loud squeal, the man laughed raucously, and then withdrew.

Her pussy ached but she wanted more – much more. And she was not to be disappointed. She sensed the head of one of the cocks touching her sex again and then, to her utmost joy, she felt the other begin to enter her anus. He gripped her hips and pushed into her in one slow and measured movement, until she accommodated both his cocks to the hilt. Sahria was in heaven. She felt so full and so complete. This was no punishment. The fact that she was shackled made his assault upon her all the more pleasurable. As far as she was concerned he could do to her whatever he wanted.

The man began to move quickly in and out of her with sharp firm jabs. Having both her pussy and her bottom fucked in such perfect unison brought her quickly once more to the point of release. She stiffened and contracted the muscles of her lower abdomen. The man sensed her imminent climax and increased his pace. He speared her at a frantic rate whilst again pawing her sweating breasts and pinching her hard nipples painfully. Her juices flooded from her engorged sex as she came, soaking her inner thighs. He continued to pound in and out of her two holes rapidly until her moans of pleasure faded with the tremors of her release, and then he pulled from her.

There was a sudden gleeful cry from behind her.

Wearily, Sahria turned her head to look at Calema. The girl's face was flushed and her body coated with a sheen of fresh sweat. She had quite obviously come herself whilst merely witnessing Sahria's ecstasy. The two girls smiled at each other, and soon it would be Calema's turn to enjoy this ultimate experience.

Sahria looked at the man they called the snake. His twin stalks still stood proudly erect, their ebony skin glistening with oil and sex juices. He moved back, clearly not done with her yet. She felt the bulbous heads of his cocks touching between her buttocks and braced herself for further delights, and felt him pressing once more against her sphincter. His thumbs dug painfully into her buttocks as he pulled them apart, and she felt her anus being stretched to an impossible degree, and realised that both stiff pricks were entering her, forcing their way through the tightness. The pain was intense at first and Sahria bit her lip. Tears of anguish began to flow. 'No... no...' she cried, 'that is too much...'

But the man ignored her words and continued to force himself deep inside her bottom. She felt his belly pressing against her buttocks and knew that she had absorbed both thick stalks completely. He held still for some moments, and the pain within her bottom subsided. She felt him throb heavily inside her and wondered if, when the time came, he would shoot his cream from both angry heads.

He began to move again, cautiously at first, and Sahria was grateful for his apparent consideration. He circled his hips as if to open her more, and then started to fuck her with measured thrusts. Then she felt a stinging pain as he slapped one of her buttocks. He gripped the other buttock tightly with his free hand and slapped her again across the first. The combination of the discomfort due to the massive intrusion to her rear and the fierce blows to her bottom caused her to moan with pleasure. He began to thrust in and out of her rapidly and matched each hard jab with yet another slap on her aching buttock. The feelings of impending release built up once more inside her shuddering body. He hammered into her faster and faster. The frame to which she was shackled creaked, the wood threatening to splinter with the force of his assault. Sahria tossed her head back and screamed in joy as she came. Thoughts of Calema, the prince, Rapite, all were dismissed from her mind as she drowned in an oblivion of total bliss.

The man eased from her and she heard him pad over to where Calema was lying. Sahria was too sated and exhausted to watch the proceedings, rested her head against the gnarled wood of the frame, and closed her eyes.

The last sounds she heard as she drifted into a daze were the moans of her friend echoing around the dank cell.

Sahria lay on the softness of her large bed staring at the ornately carved ceiling. Candles burned brightly, sending flickering shadows that danced across the plasterwork. She wondered what time it was. Following their release from the black chamber they had been allowed to return to their own rooms. Calema had said nothing about their experiences with the man they called the snake. Sahria, too, had felt somewhat bemused.

She turned her head wearily. At her side lay the curled and naked form of Su-Lee, deep in slumber. Some hours before, the beautiful oriental had soothed her aching pussy and bottom with her delicate tongue, and it had been good.

Sahria raised her head and looked across the room. Calema was lying in the other bed with the twins, Shalma and Lisha. All three were asleep, a testament to their exertions over the previous couple of hours.

Su-Lee turned onto her stomach and buried her head in a pillow. Sahria looked with satisfaction at her bruised and striped bottom. The pleasure the girl took in being thrashed was astounding and yet, being mute, she barely uttered a sound no matter how fiercely she was whipped. Instead, all that could ever be heard from her was a gentle, satisfied whimper.

Sahria sat up and eased herself carefully from the bed, anxious not to disturb the sleeping girl. She slipped a robe over her nakedness and walked silently across the room, and out of the door. The passageway was deserted. Torches lit her way as she moved quickly along the corridor and out into the main hall of the palace. A group of guards, who should have been at their posts, were playing a drunken game of dice at the far end of the great room. They didn't hear her as she slipped quietly out of the main door and into the marketplace.

Apart from a couple of dogs foraging for food amongst the litter of the previous day, there was no sign of movement within the shadows of the night.

No lights burned in the windows of the buildings that surrounded her. The hour was obviously very late. The only illumination came from the moon, shining brightly in the cloudless sky.

She filled her lungs with the cool night air. It was good to be alone for once. Her loins still ached from the pummelling the tattooed man had given her, but it was a pleasant feeling. She sat on a bench and stared into the night.

'Are you feeling unwell, my lady?' The voice startled her. It came from behind and was distinctly male. She stood up swiftly and swung around, and a tall figure stood in the shadows behind her.

'Come forward, stranger,' she commanded. 'Let me see your face.'

He moved into the moonlight immediately. He was young, probably no more than eighteen. Despite his youthful looks, however, he was extremely handsome to Sahria's eyes, tall and slim but with the broad shoulders of someone well used to physical work. His complexion was heavily tanned, but his hair was as blonde as her friend Calema's, and his eyes shone a piercing blue, reflecting the silvery light of the moon. Sahria swallowed hard, feeling an almost uncontrollable and animal-like attraction to him.

'What are you doing here at this hour?' she asked, attempting to maintain a tone of authority.

The boy looked uncomfortable. 'I am merely travelling home,' he protested, walking closer to stand facing her. Being so close, she could smell the scent of his labours. The manly odour made her skin turn to gooseflesh.

'I am sorry,' she said, as she resumed her seat on the bench. 'I thought you may have been a brigand.'

He sat down next to her. 'The market is a dangerous place for a lady of such beauty to be at this hour.' He spoke softly, almost in a whisper.

Sahria turned to look at him, and their eyes met. His gaze was hypnotic, and seemed to be draining the will from her body.

'I needed some air,' she replied weakly. She shivered and pulled her robe tightly around herself, and the boy slipped an arm about her shoulders.

'You are cold, my lady,' he breathed. 'You should go back indoors.' Sahria leant her body against his. His own robe had parted slightly to reveal a muscular chest. His tanned skin was smooth and glistened in the moonlight, and there wasn't a trace of hair on his toned torso.

'I am all right,' she said, feeling oddly weak in the youth's presence, as though his sheer beauty had taken control of her senses. 'How is it that you travel so late?' she continued, anxious to conceal her feebleness.

The stranger looked oddly embarrassed, and looked down at the ground. 'I – I have been working late,' he answered lamely.

'I think it more likely that you have been visiting a lady,' she teased, and he grinned sheepishly. 'That's it, isn't it?' she pressed, and the boy nodded and then smiled as he looked into her eyes. Sahria felt a familiar sensation between her legs. The mere sight of a handsome male had instantly aroused her many times in the past, but this was somehow entirely different. She reached towards him and ran the tip of a finger

196

down the middle of his bare chest. 'She is a very lucky girl,' she said huskily.

The stranger shrugged modestly. Sahria parted his robe still more and glanced down. A small strip of linen was all that covered his genitals, and she felt her own sex begin to weep with the juices of arousal. She looked into his eyes once more. Their faces moved together slowly until their lips touched, lightly at first, and then they pressed hard against each other, their tongues darting and probing. Sahria imagined him making love to his lady. She knew his body was no doubt still aching from a host of wonderful experiences with her and yet, here he was in the arms of a complete stranger just moments after taking his leave from her.

She pulled her face from his and looked down. His cock was jutting from the barely adequate linen strip, hard and erect. She smiled. Whatever he had been doing during his clandestine meeting hadn't completely satisfied his desires. He was clearly ready for more.

The stranger suddenly saw what she was looking at and drew his cloak quickly about his body. Sahria laughed and kissed his flushed face. 'Don't be shy,' she teased. 'You have nothing to be ashamed of.' She drew back his cloak again, this time pushing it from his shoulders. She unknotted the linen pouch and gazed at his manly nakedness. His erection thrust firmly upward, almost pressing against his stomach. It was not large, but to Sahria's eyes at that moment it was the most beautiful thing she had ever seen.

She reached out and circled the rigid stalk with her fingers. He breathed in deeply as she moved her hand gently up and down. She felt his cock throb and a small drop of pre-come appeared from the slit. Bending forward, she licked the juice from him and then sat up again and gazed into his bulging eyes. There was nothing more to be said. She released her grip and drew back her cloak, allowing it to slip from her shoulders. Now they were both naked, sitting on the cool bench with the flesh of their sculptured bodies shimmering in the moonlight.

The stranger looked down at her heaving breasts, and licked his lips hungrily. Sahria felt proud; she knew that one glance at her firm globes would be enough to enslave any man. He reached out nervously and stroked one of her breasts lightly, and then caught hold of the ring piercing her erect nipple. She sighed with pleasure as he tugged it slightly, bent his head forward and kissed the nipple, then drew it between his lips and suckled her like an infant. She could feel him circling the ring with the tip of his tongue. He moved to the other breast and she reached out and grasped his stiff cock again. He put his hand on her knee and then slid it with agonising slowness up her inner thigh, and Sahria parted her legs in happy anticipation.

She felt him touch her pussy lightly, and then he pulled back suddenly and looked down. Her sex lips were engorged and the rings glinted in the moonlight. The youth reached out and touched one of the rings with the tip of his finger. It was obvious that he had never seen such a thing before. 'Beautiful,' he breathed.

'Do you like the rings?' she asked in a hushed voice.

'Beautiful,' he repeated simply. He caressed her soft

flesh gently, occasionally nipping the rings between his forefinger and thumb whilst moving his mouth back to suckle one of her nipples. Sahria moaned softly and prayed that no one would interrupt their liaison. She gripped his erection tightly as though she was afraid he would escape from her.

The stranger moved and knelt on the ground. Sahria spread her legs, offering him the most delightful view of her lush treasure. He bent forward and kissed her sex lightly, and she felt she would come immediately. Her entire body trembled as he began to run his tongue around her aching sex flesh, but his inexperience showed in the way he barely made contact with her throbbing little bud. She reached down and pulled her lips apart with her fingers, guiding him, and he dipped his tongue into the juicy entrance.

Sahria stiffened, but for some unaccountable reason she couldn't push herself into blissful release. Undaunted, she pushed the stranger's head away and motioned for him to stand, and then stroked his chest and stomach with both hands.

She eyed the perfection of his lithe body with more than a little satisfaction. His turgid cock stood fiercely erect, spearing proudly from his groin.

Sahria reached out and took hold of his stiff rod, and took it immediately into the wet warmth of her mouth. She enveloped the column of flesh quickly, taking it to the back of her throat, then moved her head back slowly until just the head was held within the luscious cushion of her lips. She ran her tongue around it and traced the shape of the deep ridge. The young man groaned and she moved her head back quickly in order to let him slip from her.

'Don't come yet,' she warned. 'Not until you've fucked me.'

The stranger shook his head. 'No, no, I'm all right,' he panted, although it was apparent that he was anything but all right. Sahria knew she would have to be careful. She was fully aware of the effect her oral ministrations could have on a rampant erection, but she also loved the feel and taste of it in her mouth.

She leaned forward while gripping his cock tightly at the root. Opening her mouth she took him between her lips once more and lapped hungrily at his stiffness with her tongue. She could taste the sweet flavour of pussy on his hard flesh. It hadn't been long since he had impaled his lover, and doubtless come inside her. Perhaps, in view of that, he would be able to control himself.

She let go of his cock and gripped his buttocks, forcing him to push his erection fully inside her mouth while she arched her neck and took him down her throat until his pubic bone pressed against her lips. He groaned again and she eased back until he slipped from her. Perhaps not, she thought. She glanced up at his face, and it was clear from his pained expression that he was endeavouring to hold back an impending orgasm.

Sahria squeezed the glans tightly between her thumb and forefinger. She wasn't going to be denied. She felt him throb against the tip of her thumb, a threatening pulse, but then he relaxed. The urgency had passed.

She let go of him and stood, curled her arms around

his neck and pulled his mouth to hers. They kissed, and then she turned her back to him and bent over. Resting her arms on the bench, she arched her back and presented her bottom with her legs slightly bent and spread apart. The young man wasted no time. Within seconds she felt him pressing the head of his cock against her sex, and then he slid effortlessly inside her until his groin pressed against her buttocks. His size was nothing compared to what she had endured during the past few days, but it was most pleasurable.

He moved slowly at first, with perfect rhythm, occasionally circling his hips so his shaft rubbed firmly against the rings that pierced her labia. Then he began to move faster, his groin slapping noisily against her bottom.

Sahria lifted her head and gazed into the darkness as the panting youth hammered harder and harder against her, and suddenly she realised they were being watched. She peered into the night and saw a solitary soldier, masturbating openly as he enjoyed the spectacle. She wanted to call him over to join them, so she could take him in her mouth and allow him to fill her throat with his cream, but she thought better of it. She didn't want to scare her young lover away with a display of such wantonness, and above all, she badly needed to come.

Gripping the bench with one hand she felt between her legs and rubbed furiously, but still to no avail.

The young man must have taken her actions as some sort of encouragement for he started to slap wildly against her, pounding is weapon in and out of her like a man possessed. Sahria heard a groan and looked up to see the watching soldier's cream erupting from his cock to stream wastefully onto the stony ground, and then her lover joined him in blissful release. His stalk pumped and he grunted as he filled her with his juices. Sahria burst into tears of frustration and pulled from him. Grabbing her robe, she ran sobbing past the guard and back into the palace, leaving a bemused but sated young man standing in the marketplace.

Sahria lay alone on her bed, once more staring at the ornate ceiling. Why hadn't she come? What was wrong with her? The young man had been handsome, with a perfect body and a beautiful cock. Normally she would have orgasmed freely in such an erotic situation.

She looked across at Calema's bed. Her friend was lying asleep with one of the twins sprawled between her legs, and with her head buried in the softness of Calema's crotch. The other twin was sitting with her back resting against the head of the bed, looking across at her through the shadows of the night. The girl smiled, and Sahria beckoned her over. Dutifully, she left Calema's side and padded across the room. Sahria opened her legs and the girl immediately knelt between them and began to lap her. Sahria came instantly. She gasped and thrust her hips upwards, almost nudging the twin from the bed. The girl sat up and looked at her in surprise, her beautiful face soaked with Sahria's juices. Sahria dismissed her abruptly with a wave of a hand, and the twin returned petulantly to Calema's bed.

Sahria turned her back on the others and curled into an embryonic position. For a few moments it occurred to her that perhaps she could only find sexual satisfaction with others of her own sex, but she dismissed the thought from her mind. She knew she loved the sight of a man's naked body, and the taste of his cock. And the thought of never enjoying the feel of a stiff erection or two pounding in and out of her was preposterous.

She ran a hand absently over the plump curve of her buttocks, and traced the welts that still marked her soft skin. Closing her eyes, she remembered the blissful pain she'd experienced when the lash struck her, and a realisation dawned.

The pain!

The young man's gentle, albeit persuasive lovemaking had been wasted on her. She needed to feel the delightful agony of pain!

If the young man had somehow shackled her to the bench in the marketplace, and perhaps the watching soldier had whipped her soundly while she was fucked, she knew she would have come over and over again.

Sahria closed her eyes and pictured the scene. She touched herself between the legs and knew it was true. She knew now that her future delights would be as a result of total subservience to her master or mistress.

Princess Sahria had become a slave – a slave to the delights of pain and submission.

Chapter Ten

The sounds coming from the other side of the dormitory door were unmistakable. There were male grunts and girlish squeals coupled with the rhythmic panting of strenuous lovemaking. Sahria stood for a moment and listened, a knowing grin on her face. It was still quite early in the morning, and yet her pupils were already indulging in the delights of the pink chamber.

'I'm coming… I'm coming…'

Sahria recognised the cries of joy as being those of Mena, a virgin just seven days previously. The girls had certainly learnt their lessons well over the last week. She and Calema had instructed them in every diversion they knew and, to their surprise, had learnt many things themselves. As she continued to eavesdrop she conjured up a mental picture of Mena's lovely body impaled on the stalk of a rampant lover, and the image excited her immensely.

She opened the door quietly and slipped into the room. The eight small beds seemed to be covered by a sea of writhing nakedness. There must have been fifteen or possibly even twenty men enjoying the maidens, and the scent in the room was a strong mixture of sweat and female arousal, that Sahria found immediately intoxicating.

It was apparent from the clothing strewn around the room that the men were soldiers, and it occurred to her to wonder just who was guarding the palace at that moment. She recognised most of them; many had been instrumental in the girls' tuition.

Zia was on the bed nearest to her. The ebony beauty was lying astride one man, while another was squatting behind her with his cock firmly embedded in her bottom. A third soldier was feeding her suckling mouth with his equally stiff erection.

Next to her, Mena was lying exhausted on her bed with her lover's head between her thighs, her eyes glazed and her face flushed as testament to her recent orgasm.

As was their wont, the twins Shalma and Lisha were pleasuring a single young man, who they merely required to lie on his back while they worked on his genitals with their tongues.

Jo-Jo had been tied by her wrists to the head of her bed. She was kneeling with her bottom presented in the most blatant fashion, and a small procession of men took it in turn to impale her luscious treasures.

Su-Lee was in a similar position, sucking an erection while two other soldiers were caning her bottom with thin switches. Sahria couldn't help but question the wisdom of the guard the oriental was sucking. A more stinging cut from one of the canes would surely cause her to sink her teeth into his vulnerable flesh.

But it was Aisha who presented the most erotic sight. The petit blonde could barely be seen under the writhing mass of male bodies that seemed to be swamping her like some monster from the annals of mythology. She was lying in a similar position to that adopted by Zia, her slim legs stretched over the supine form of one man, who was thrusting his cock into her pussy while another erection plundered the forbidden depths of her bottom. Two men knelt before her face and, incredibly, she was managing to accommodate both of them in her mouth. Two more guards stood on either side of the bed and she was clutching their erections, gently rubbing them up and down. The final two men stood at the base of the bed and were using her dainty feet to masturbate.

Yes, thought Sahria, her pupils had learnt their lessons well. They were ready for the prince's pleasure. She slipped silently out of the door, happy to leave the girls to their pursuits of pleasure, and headed back to the blue chamber.

It was as she entered her room that she suddenly realised she hadn't seen Agita, but assumed her charge must be in the company of the prince. For some reason Sarne seemed to have a preference for the girl. It appeared strange to Sahria that it should be so; Agita was facially lovely, but her body was plumper than the others, albeit in a voluptuous way. Nevertheless, Prince Sarne had called her to his chambers on no less than four occasions during the past week.

Sahria felt a pang of envy. Apart from the wonderful time in the marketplace, the prince hadn't approached her in any way, and she yearned to feel him ploughing into her once again.

And so she decided; he had teased her for long enough – it was time for action.

Sahria had selected her clothing carefully, determined that the prince should not reject her advances. She'd chosen a basque of soft black leather that hugged her sumptuous form tightly, her nipples visible through two convenient holes cut into the garment. She had removed the small rings that usually adorned her nipples, and replaced them with larger ones.

To each of these rings she'd attached a long length of chain, which hung tantalisingly from the swell of her breasts. Two further lengths of chain circled her upper thighs, linking to the tiny rings that pierced her labia.

She turned and glanced over her shoulder at her reflection in a mirror. Her rounded bottom was bare, and the marks of previous chastisements had all but faded from her smooth skin. It had been too long for her. She needed to feel the sweet kiss of the switch again, very soon.

Her outfit was completed by a pair of thigh-length leather boots with tall heels; she was not going to be denied this time.

She called two guards and asked that they take her to the prince. By the time they reached his quarters she was almost breathless with sexual anticipation. The door opened and the two men guided her into the room, and Sahria gasped at what she saw.

Agita was lying on a bed with a cushion under her shoulders and her head strained back. Sarne was positioned with his knees on either side of her shoulders, his cock embedded in the girl's mouth. The guards and Sahria watched in fascination as the prince fucked Agita's throat.

Suddenly he became aware that he had visitors, and withdrew from Agita's mouth and slipped from the bed. He stood glaring at Sahria, his cock slowly beginning to wilt, and hanging heavily from his groin. 'What do you want?' he barked angrily.

Sahria bowed subserviently. 'You are the prince, my lord,' she replied. 'It is for you to say what you require of me.'

'Can't you see that I am otherwise occupied? Are you blind?'

Sahria began to tremble at the fury in his tone, and became angry with herself. Was she not a powerful woman? Had she not thrashed the girls into submission? She took a deep breath and held herself proudly. 'My lord,' she said, 'I can see that one of my pupils has been giving you pleasure. But I have been patient, Prince Sarne. I have trained the girls and they are all ready to serve you. Now I demand my reward, as you promised.'

Sarne strode quickly to stand face to face with her, his eyes blazing. 'Demand?' he spat, his voice almost cracking with fury. 'You dare to demand? You are a princess of pleasure, here only to do my bidding without question!' He grabbed the two chains clamped to her nipple rings and tugged, pulling her harshly towards him. Sahria yelped with the sudden pain. 'You are a woman; your position in my court is to be beaten and fucked by me or any other person I choose. Nothing more! Do you understand?'

Sahria found the cruelty of his words strangely exhilarating, and bowed deferentially. 'Yes, my lord,' she said, with deliberate subservience in her tone. The prince tugged the chains again, and Sahria bit her bottom lip to stop herself from crying out.

He smiled, but there was no trace of kindness in his expression. She glanced down submissively and saw, to her delight, that his cock was once more erect. But to her profound disappointment the prince stepped back, looked at her disapprovingly, and then walked to the far side of the room, his cock waving as he moved. He turned to face her again. 'You will be taken to the great hall, then stripped and shackled to a bench,' he announced. 'You will remain there for twenty-four hours with neither food nor drink. Anyone who sees you there may use you as he or she pleases.

'Once this period is over I will come to you and thrash you severely. Perhaps then you will know your place and regret your impertinence.' He turned to face one of the servants. 'See that she is suitably restrained,' he ordered.

The servants immediately dragged her out of the room and back into the passageway. The door was slammed behind them and, almost immediately she heard Agita's muffled giggle from within.

If the prince's words had been meant as a threat to terrify Sahria, they didn't have the desired effect. Despite the fact that she was being roughly forced to move quickly along the passageway towards the great hall, she nevertheless became more and more excited at the prospect of being shackled and abused for so long. And, of course, she was certain that this time the prince would keep his promise...

The servants did their work well. They saw to it that Sahria was sprawled naked and face down across a bench, with her arms and legs spread on either side and her wrists and ankles securely manacled to the four corners. A cushion had been placed under her groin, not necessarily to offer her some comfort, but to raise her bottom so that her pussy could be seen by anyone standing behind her. The chains attached to her labia were left in place, as were those fixed to her nipple rings. These last chains were tugged tightly and wound around the front legs of the bench, causing her nipples to be stretched painfully.

Their work done, the two men stood and looked down on her prone form contemptuously. She raised her head and glared back at them with equal distaste. One of the men pulled back his loincloth and revealed his thickening tool. It seemed clear to her what his intentions were. The other man followed suit, and then the pair moved behind her so that she was unable to see what they were doing.

She waited for the inevitable prodding at her pussy lips, but instead they oiled her bottom and upper thighs.

Then, upon hearing familiar rhythmic sounds, she strained to glance over her shoulder, and saw both men, rather than using her vulnerability in the way she craved, content to masturbate whilst gazing at her tethered form. Sahria felt humiliated in the extreme, but remained silent. She would not beg, and certainly not of servants.

A few seconds later she felt a warm spray across the tender skin of her bottom as one and then the other ejaculated. The men sniggered disdainfully, and having taken their pleasure, walked off, leaving her to her fate.

It was not long before Sahria heard footsteps; her ordeal was about to begin!

She raised her head as best she could. There seemed to be dozens of people entering the hall, and she guessed the two servants would have ensured that word of her plight got around the court very quickly. The people began to chatter excitedly. There were both male and female voices, some of which she recognised. This was far more degrading than what had happened in the marketplace. At least there the people couldn't see her face and she couldn't see them, and they had been strangers of the city. This time most of the onlookers would be people she knew, and many of them would have suffered at her hands in the past. Now they had the opportunity to wreak their revenge, and she was certain they would not shrink from the task.

The people crowded around her, like curious children seeing a curious animal for the first time. Somebody touched her bottom and she shuddered involuntarily. Somebody else slipped two or three fingers inside her pussy. 'She is as wet as a whore's mouth!' exclaimed a male voice.

'She's no better than a whore herself,' said a woman venomously. The crowd laughed. More fingers probed her roughly, two or possibly three different hands exploring her juicy depths simultaneously, and she secretly ached for a cock to plunge into her to sate her rising lust.

'Lash the bitch!' someone yelled, and his cry was taken up immediately by others in the rabid mass.

Sahria closed her eyes and waited for the pain. She

detected a familiar scent and opened them again. An erection was inches from her mouth, the owner kneeling in front of her face. She could have raised her head and looked to see who it was, but it somehow didn't seem to matter, so she parted her lips and engulfed the stalk. Whoever it was came immediately and bathed the back of her throat, and she swallowed the cream gratefully.

The man slipped his drooping phallus from between her pouting lips. A thin trail of his juice hung between it and her lips like a strand of spider's silk.

Then she heard a swish and felt a stinging pain as a cane cut her across both buttocks. She was thankful the man had come when he did, for she would certainly have bitten into his cock with the shock of the blow if he hadn't. The crowd cheered and a second stroke was delivered, this time across the lower part of her bottom. But the third cut was the worst, she howled, and the crowd cheered again.

The pain was agonising. Whoever was caning her either hated her or simply relished the task. Three more strokes were delivered with somewhat less severity, until her tormentor tired and she heard the cane fall to the marble floor, and numerous hands mauled her bottom, as if to feel her pain.

Sahria felt utterly degraded, knowing that her debasement had barely begun. Fingers once more probed her pussy, and then one prodded clumsily into her anus, causing her to tense with the pain.

Gradually, however, her muscles relaxed and she welcomed two and then three fingers into her tight sphincter. She felt her clitoris throb and knew she was going to come. She feared what they might do if she showed any pleasure, but there was nothing she could do to stop it. The incessant clawing at her sex was driving her to distraction, and suddenly she lost control completely, raised her head and screamed as the orgasm ripped through her.

'The little slut's come,' a woman declared, and the crowd jeered.

'Fuck her!' called another.

'Yeah, fuck her till she can take no more!'

'Fuck her! Fuck her!' The demand turned into a chant, and Sahria trembled.

'She's terrified!' somebody exclaimed gleefully, but it couldn't have been further from the truth; Sahria could not possibly have been more aroused.

And her wish was granted almost immediately. The hands slipped from her, all apart from the finger probing her anus. She waited in eager anticipation, and after a short pause she felt the rubbery head of a stiff penis touching her aching cunt and, in the next moment it was inside her to the hilt. Whoever it was began to thrust rapidly. He gripped her thighs tightly and dug his fingernails into her flesh as he hammered his groin against her bottom. There was no consideration for her in the man's violent abuse of her body, but she loved it. She would take them all. She would not be overcome.

Another fine erection was presented to her face. Sahria opened her mouth and the stranger pushed forward until she was forced to take his substantial weapon down her throat. Always happy to perform such a task, she swallowed repeatedly in the knowledge that her actions would give him the most delightful sensations as her throat muscles undulated along the length of his stalk. She wanted to enhance her oral caress by cupping his balls, but her shackles prevented it. All she could do was concentrate on pleasuring him with her mouth.

Sahria used her substantial expertise in the art of fellatio and the man came within moments. She felt his cock throbbing within her throat and avidly swallowed his cream. 'The bitch is draining me...' she heard him groan. 'She's sucking me dry...'

The scene must have had an effect on the man pummelling her pussy for he, too, cried out in blissful release and ejaculated. Having two men come inside her simultaneously had always delighted Sahria, and this coupled with another person expertly frigging her arse was so exhilarating that she joined them in a joyous climax.

Eventually they withdrew, and Sahria eagerly awaited her next intrusion.

Whoever had been fingering her bottom also left her, and she felt once more delightfully vulnerable.

'Thrash the slut again!' cried another female voice.

'Let me do it!' pleaded a man. 'I want to slap that arse!'

Sahria felt the first stinging blow of a rough hand as it slapped her right buttock. The second smack hit her other rounded globe.

'Look at it quiver!' The tone of the voice was filled with lust and cruelty, and it pleased her. More blows were administered in rapid succession, making it obvious to her that more than one person was engaged in her humiliation.

The beating continued for quite some time. It seemed that everyone wanted to take his or her turn to slap her. The sounds of flesh smacking flesh echoed around the great hall like an erotic symphony, and Sahria came again.

Eventually the crowd tired and the slaps ceased. Somebody ejaculated over her bottom. Three more men took their turns to fuck her, and then the people drifted away to enjoy their own libidinous pursuits in private.

Chapter Eleven

Sahria awoke slowly from a long and fitful sleep. She had been dreaming of the prince, and it had all seemed so very real, but as the mists of slumber cleared, she realised she was numb, and aching intensely. She heard voices and sighed. The thought of having to endure more physical abasement filled her with despair.

A group of old women studied her, and Sahria felt dirty and degraded. They talked quietly amongst themselves and shook their heads, and she wondered what they intended to do with her.

One of the group bent and began to unclasp the shackle that secured her wrist to the leg of bench. The other women followed their colleague's example, and once Sahria's other limbs were free they carefully unclasped the chains from her nipple rings and helped her to a sitting position. Sahria flopped against one of them, with her head against the woman's ample chest, and the woman stroked her tousled hair.

'Come, princess,' she whispered. 'We must bathe you.'

The milky water of the bath felt blissfully soothing as it washed over Sahria's tortured flesh. The old women busied themselves about her, and she watched in a daze as they prepared silky garments for her to wear, the steam rising from the hot bath giving them a ghostly appearance. There was a sense of unreality about it all, and Sahria wondered briefly if she was still dreaming.

She was washed gently and thoroughly, and then left to soak in the hot bath alone.

The scent of the water filled her nostrils and she closed her eyes and lay back to relax in the gentle ambience of the moment. She began to think about the events of the previous night, the thrashings, the constant sex, and above all, the humiliation.

Two of the old women returned carrying bundles of towels. They helped Sahria out of the bath and dried her, then as one of them brushed her long hair, the other carefully clipped her pubic hair neatly. Sahria still felt dazed from her recent experiences, and watched dispassionately as the woman worked deftly.

She was then made to lie on a table, which had been covered by a silken sheet. Two more of the women returned to the room, each of them carrying a silver jug. They stood on either side of her and one of them poured warm oil over her body, while the other female massaged it into her skin. Sahria closed her eyes and relaxed. For once her thoughts were not dominated by libidinous dreams, despite their intimate caresses. The women oiled her breasts and ran their slippery fingers between her thighs, although they avoided touching her newly clipped pubis. She breathed the perfumed air gently and the aches in her limbs faded under their expert ministrations.

She was made to lie on her stomach, the second jug of oil was poured over her, and the women stroked her smooth back, her thighs and her calves. Sahria parted her legs a little and they smoothed the insides of her upper thighs, and then concentrated their attentions on her tortured bottom.

'What a whipping you must have taken, princess,' said one of the women, as she caressed the soft globes. Sahria could feel their fingertips tracing the lines of the raised welts, but there was no discomfort; the awful stinging had dissipated.

'Such a beautiful, beautiful bottom,' breathed another. Sahria felt her run her fingertips down the cleft between her buttocks and, for a moment, hoped she would touch her pussy, which was rapidly becoming oiled with juices of her own. Instead, though, the woman smoothed both hands across Sahria's buttocks while her companion massaged her thighs again.

'The marks are nearly gone,' said the first woman. 'The oil has worked well.'

'The prince will be pleased,' said the other. 'He likes to tan a nice fresh backside.'

Sahria suddenly realised what was happening. She was being prepared for him. The prince was going to keep his word, and she vowed that this time she would use every skill she had ever learned to make him realise that she was indeed the true princess of pleasure!

Their task completed, the women guided Sahria to her feet. One of them brushed her hair again briefly and tidied it over her shoulders, while the other slipped a diaphanous silk robe about her nakedness. Sahria glanced at her reflection in a nearby mirror. The robe covered her body from neck to her feet, but the silk was so fine that the garment was virtually transparent, and highlighted the shapely contours of her body to perfection. She stood proudly erect, her breasts thrusting magnificently, her nipples and their golden adornments clearly visible.

The women held her hands and led her gently from the room, and Sahria felt extremely nervous as they walked down the long passageway towards the prince's chambers.

They reached the door, and one of the women knocked. The door was opened and Sahria was surprised to see the naked form of Mena standing there. The girl stepped aside, bowed low, and they entered the opulent room. Aisha, the blonde nymphet, was lying naked on the huge bed. Clearly the prince had already been savouring her delights. Sahria felt disappointed and somewhat slighted; she had wanted the prince to herself.

There was no sign of Sarne. Sahria was led to the bed and made to slip out of the robe. Aisha moved to the side of the bed and invitingly smoothed a hand across the sheet next to her. Sahria slipped onto the bed and lay next to her, feeling a little bemused. Mena joined them and the old women left the room, quietly closing the door behind them.

Sahria lay on her back staring at the ornate ceiling, feeling very disheartened. It appeared that her role was merely to be just one of three lovers for the insatiable prince. She looked at Mena, and then turned to face Aisha. Both girls were lying on their sides facing her, their eyes shining with lust.

'Where is Prince Sarne?' Sahria asked.

'He will return soon,' whispered Aisha. 'We have

been instructed to prepare you for him.'

'What do you mean?' Sahria was angry at the girl's impertinence. It was hardly her pupils' place to prepare her for anything.

'You have taught us well, mistress,' said Mena, in her hushed tones. 'The prince is a very demanding lover. He has ordered that you be fully aroused before he takes you.'

Sahria calmed herself, finding her words unsurprising. Sarne no doubt felt it would be too demeaning for him to be bothered to stimulate and seduce her. The girls would do the work for him, he would then fuck her, and after sating himself he would leave her.

Mena moved closer and stroked her breasts. Sahria relaxed, ready to enjoy the stimulating experience of gentle feminine caresses. Aisha ran her hand over Sahria's stomach and then down to cup her mound, and Sahria felt the girl's middle finger slip between her sex lips.

'You are already very wet,' Aisha breathed. 'There seems little need for us to arouse you.'

'Nevertheless,' Sahria sighed, 'you must do as the prince has ordered.'

The two girls bent to her, and each took a nipple in her mouth and playfully licked around the gold rings that pierced the erect buds. Mena slipped her hand between Sahria's legs and both girls fingered her expertly. They were right; she had taught them well. Their touch was heavenly. She felt her sex lips open and her oily juice soak their probing fingers. Spreading her legs, she rested them across the girls, and they slipped more fingers inside her while still sucking her nipples.

Aisha reached over to a bedside table and picked up a small jug. She poured the viscous contents over her hand and then set the jug down again. It was clear what she intended to do. Sahria raised her legs and rested her knees against her breasts. Aisha prodded at her tight anus, and then the girl slipped a couple of fingers in to the knuckle. Sahria gasped with delight, and Aisha slowly pushed all four fingers into her bottom, bunching them tightly together.

Mena was continuing to stimulate her mistress' clutching sex, driving Sahria to the brink of orgasm, and the blissful sensations caused by Aisha's rhythmic penetration of her bottom served to heighten the pleasure almost beyond measure.

The two girls worked steadily to open and relax Sahria in readiness for their master. Sahria let her mind wander, with thoughts of rampant cocks and slippery tongues, drifting on a cloud of ecstasy. She dreamily pinched her nipples and tugged the rings that pierced them.

'I'm coming...' she panted. 'Oh, I'm *coming...*' Rhythmic wet sounds filled her ears as she was carried over the pinnacle of ultimate joy. There was a crescendo of ecstatic sensations that rushed her body, a seemingly endless climax of countless delights.

'Ohhh...' she panted, as the feelings began to subside.

Aisha and Mena slipped from the bed, and Sahria relaxed.

'Have we served you well, mistress?' Mena asked.

'Yes, you have both served me perfectly. Go and tell the prince I am ready for him.'

The two lovely girls disappeared, and after a few minutes the door opened. Sahria held her breath as a tall hooded figure entered, his body entirely swathed in a long black cloak. Her first thought was that it was the one they called the snake. She raised her head and tried to see his face, but he removed the hood and Sahria smiled as she gazed upon the cruel but handsome features of Prince Sarne.

'Well, my princess of pleasure,' he said slowly, 'do you feel suitably humbled after last night?'

'Yes, my lord,' she replied in an acquiescent tone, and he moved to stand at the foot of the bed.

'I am going to fuck you like you have never been fucked before,' he announced. Sahria nodded slowly in response. 'Now stand up,' he ordered.

Sahria slipped from the bed and stood naked before him. She was shaking, but it was lust not fear that made her tremble. He cupped her firm breasts and pushed his thumbs through her nipple rings. 'You have a beautiful body, princess,' he said quietly.

'Thank you, my lord,' she replied, her mouth dry with emotion. He bent his head and kissed each of her nipples in turn, and then took his hands from her breasts and raised himself to his full height.

'Turn around,' he ordered, she obeyed instantly, and he stroked her bottom gently. 'Your skin is barely marked,' he said. 'The oil has worked well.' He fondled her with both hands, and then pinched one of her buttocks sharply. 'Perhaps a little thrashing might not go amiss,' he whispered.

'Whatever my lord pleases,' she replied coyly, determined to conceal the fact that she was yearning for the stinging slap of his hand on her bottom. The prince moved from her and sat on the edge of the bed.

'Come across me,' he ordered. Sahria lay over his knees with her bottom raised and her hands and toes resting on the floor. 'Such a perfect arse,' he muttered, as he ran a hand over her soft skin, and eased a finger into her anus. 'You have been prepared well.'

Sahria could feel the hardness of his cock under her stomach, and then he slapped her bottom and she yelped. Her cry was more from surprise than pain, but it seemed to please him, for he laughed and slapped her again. She gasped; it hurt, but the pain only served to heighten her lust.

'You know you have been a very wicked girl,' he said as he slapped her quivering buttocks three more times.

'Yes, my lord,' she panted in reply. 'Very wicked.' She didn't know which particular misdemeanour he was referring to, but it didn't matter. More sharp blows followed, administered alternately to each buttock. Her bottom began to sting and the juices flowed from her oiled pussy. A final slap was delivered, and then the prince pushed her roughly to the floor.

'See that you do not misbehave in the future,' he snapped as he glared down at her.

'Yes, my lord,' she said, her head bowed in subservience. He unfastened his cloak and let it fall from his shoulders to reveal his muscular nakedness, his cock rising in all its magnificence from his bushy groin.

'Suck it,' he commanded.

Sahria moved forward on her knees and grasped the monster with both hands. She massaged his flesh and put her lips to the bulbous head, kissed it lightly, and then opened her mouth wide to engulf it. She took as much of his length as she could while still gripping the long stalk, and he groaned as she lapped his glans with the flat of her tongue. He had the taste and scent of female release on his flesh.

Sahria moved her head back and let him slip from her mouth. She gripped the root tightly, leant forward, licked up and down the length, and then ran her tongue over his balls. She took one and then both of the orbs into her mouth and sucked the loose flesh, whilst once more rubbing her hands up and down his cock.

She felt him throb within her tight grip and a sliver of pre-come oozed from the slit and slipped slowly down his length. Sahria let his balls fall from her mouth and licked the cream from the gnarled stem, then once more engulfed the purple head.

But without warning he pulled her by the hair and wrenched her head back. Sahria looked up at him, worried that she had displeased him in some way, but he smiled kindly. She was shocked; it was the first time he had ever looked at her in such a way, and it confused her.

'You will have me finishing before I have started,' he said.

Sahria bowed her head. 'I am sorry, my lord.'

'There is no need for apology,' he said. 'Lie on the bed.'

Sahria slipped obediently onto the bed, and lay on

her back with her legs together and her body slightly curled. She eyed him provocatively as he rose to his feet. He stood for a moment, his cock jutting forward menacingly.

'You really are beautiful,' he repeated, and Sahria averted her gaze with unaccustomed coyness.

The prince joined her on the bed and lay by her side. He took her into his arms and their mouths met. Sahria hugged him tightly, and could feel his erection pressing hard against her stomach as she ran her hands down his broad back and stroked his taut buttocks. Their tongues darted against each other as they kissed.

Sarne moved to kneel at her side, bent over and licked around one of her breasts, tracing its shape with the tip of his tongue. A hand slipped between her legs and he began to caress her wet pussy, as he took one of her nipples in his mouth. He sucked gently at first, flicking the ring with his tongue. She moaned softly, and he slipped two fingers between the lips of her sex and fed them deep into the oily sheath. He moved down her body, licking constantly until his face was pressed against her wet pubic mound.

Sahria grasped his cock and rubbed him gently. She was already close to her orgasm as she pressed her pubic bone against him and moaned softly. Sensing her need, he moved his tongue to her erect little bud, flicked the tip rapidly over the sensitive flesh, and she came almost immediately.

The prince then moved around her without once taking his tongue from her oily cunt, until he lay between her legs with his face buried in the softness of her groin. He licked around her lips for a few moments, and then gripped her clitoris gently between his teeth. He flicked the tip of his tongue from side to side and she knew she was coming again. The orgasm tore through her, causing her to whimper with joy.

Sarne raised his head and knelt between her legs, looking at her with a wolfish smile. He lay by her side, taking her once more into his arms, and kissed her lightly on the forehead. His unaccustomed tenderness confused her. She had been used and abused at his orders by so many, and yet now he was making affectionate love to her, and she began to wonder if he had developed feelings other than pure lust.

His cock lay heavily on his stomach, and unable to resist, she reached out and gripped it, and it stiffened rapidly until it had regained its former magnificence.

The prince again moved to kneel between her legs. She raised her knees, and he shuffled closer. She knew Mena and Aisha had prepared her well, and she relaxed and waited for the ultimate penetration. He slid slowly into her, three or four inches at first, and then withdrew until her stretched pussy lips gripped him under the ridge. Then he moved into her again, slowly, before once more withdrawing. She glanced down between her legs. It was so large and so beautiful, and she needed it all.

Sarne rested his fists on either side of her, paused for a few moments, then sank his entire length into her. She squealed with delight as waves of pleasurable pain coursed throughout her body. He held still for a moment, and then began to steadily fuck her with long, slow strokes. The feeling of his enormous shaft stretching and thrusting deep inside her body thrilled her immensely, and she responded by bucking her hips upward to meet his urgent movements. Sensing her need, he hammered into her as deeply as he could, and then circled his hips to probe every part of her tight honeypot, sometimes hurting her but always delighting her.

With each deep prod against her tender flesh she rose nearer and nearer to yet another orgasm. When she finally came she clawed at his back, tearing at his sinewy flesh with her fingernails, oblivious to any pain she might be causing him. The prince responded by thrusting violently and using his size to great effect. Sahria's breasts bounced on her chest in time with his persistent pounding, and her breathing came in short sharp gasps.

Eventually he slowed his movements and raised himself. Kneeling between her legs, he gripped her ankles and fucked her slowly whilst watching in fascination as his engorged tool ploughed in and out of her clutching cunt. After a while he moved her leg across his body and wriggled around in order to lie on his side behind her. She arched her back and thrust her bottom out, and he began to steadily slip in and out of her while tickling her clitoris with his fingertips.

Sahria had never known such ecstasy. She peered over her shoulder at her lover. 'Do you want to fuck my bottom, my lord?' she whispered hoarsely.

The prince said nothing, but pulled from her and guided her onto all fours. Then he knelt behind her, and she felt the prodding of his stiff penis against her dark little sphincter.

It hurt slightly as he pushed into her, but the oil and Aisha's expert preparation served her well. She closed her eyes and moaned softly as he fed more and more of his length cautiously into her bottom, until his hairy groin pressed against the rounded cheeks of her buttocks. He began by slowly moving his hips, and then gradually but steadily increased his pace until he was thrusting aggressively into her, her nipples rubbing in unison with his movements against the bed. The prince gripped her waist tightly, and then she suddenly experienced a sharp pain as he slapped her buttock hard.

'Yes...' she urged. 'Beat me...' and the prince happily obliged.

He slapped her buttocks over and over again, and then plunged his cock in to the hilt and roared through clenched teeth. Sahria came with him, the two of them lost in an oblivion of ecstatic release. She could feel the monster throbbing inside her bottom as his cream filled her, and the sensation caused her to climax yet again. She bit the pillow beneath her face and sobbed with the sheer joy of the moment.

At last he withdrew from her, and she gazed up at him through misty eyes. He was covered with sweat and breathing heavily. 'Thank you, my lord,' she said, lowering her eyes respectfully.

Chapter Twelve

Sahria opened the door to the blue chamber carefully. It was late and she didn't want to wake Calema. The room was dark and silent. She closed the door quietly and crept over to her friend's bed, and it came as no surprise to find the young blonde curled up between the delightfully naked forms of two handsome youths, all three of them enjoying the slumber of sated exhaustion.

Calema looked so beautiful lying there, with her gentle curves and flawless white skin, and her long golden hair cascading over her slim shoulders. Sahria could imagine the apparently innocent girl sandwiched between the thrusting bodies of her two lovers, but knew that no matter how much pleasure her friend had enjoyed, it could not possibly compare with the joys she had just experienced with the prince.

The man had been insatiable, somehow managing to maintain an almost permanent erection. Eventually it had been too much for her, and she knew she had to rest.

Sahria crawled onto her bed and collapsed face down on the silken sheets. As she drifted into welcome sleep she swore she would repay the prince. Together with Calema and her eight pupils she would give him a time he would never forget.

It was noon when she finally awoke. Calema and her two lovers had gone, probably to join the other girls in the pink chambers. Sahria sat up and stretched, slipped from the bed and headed into an adjoining room to wash, and then returned to the bedroom.

Her thoughts turned to the prince. She had been planning something special for some time by way of proving to him that she was worthy of his trust. The girls had all been instructed well, and Sahria was confident they would not let her down.

Sahria dressed in a simple flowing robe and headed quickly for the pink chambers, where she found the girls and gathered them around.

'You have learnt much over these long and arduous days,' she said. 'There is no sexual delight or deviation that you have not enjoyed and would not willingly submit to again. Tonight I will present you all to the prince and the full court, and there you must prove your worth. You will all accede to whatever is demanded.' She regarded the lovely faces carefully. 'Do you understand?' she asked. The girls nodded, their eyes sparkling, and Sahria smiled proudly.

'First, there will be a race,' she went on.

'A race?' queried Su-Lee.

'You will see,' Sahria teased. 'Now you must all go and prepare yourselves. You will bathe and dowse your bodies with scented oils. You will be naked when you finally present yourselves to me for inspection, save for a thick chain that will be drawn tightly about your waists to signify your total subservience. Now go.'

The girls scurried quickly to their dormitory, closing the door behind them.

'A race?' Calema asked.

Sahria merely smiled. 'As I said to the girls, you will see.'

Sahria stood facing the crowded court feeling excitedly nervous. The prince was sitting in his normal position on the high throne. For once his groin was covered, but Sahria remembered his superb nakedness and felt her arousal growing already. His power over her was complete, but she was unsure whether it was his amazing sexual prowess that had captured her heart, or if there was something more.

She had dressed in the severest of outfits; a restrictive leather basque, festooned with bronze studs and decorated with silver chains. Her breasts were bare and her nipples were linked by another chain. Her pants were made of soft but extremely tight-fitting rubber, with a hole neatly cut at the front to reveal her sex lips, the tiny rings that pierced them glinting in the bright sunlight streaming through the many tall archways bordering the great hall. What couldn't be seen was the stubby phallus attached to the pants, which was snugly in her bottom and moved sensuously inside her whenever she moved.

Her boots were also of leather and stretched to the tops of her thighs, and she carried a heavy whip with at least a dozen long lashes.

Calema stood at her side. Her friend had again chosen to cover her entire body in figure-hugging black rubber although, this time she had declined to wear the hood, preferring instead to allow her long blonde tresses to cascade over her shoulders. She too held a whip, and was playing the strands of leather across the palm of her hand.

The prince regarded Sahria, and she noticed him stroke the bulge between his legs and felt justifiably proud of her appearance.

'My lord Sarne,' she began, 'and people of the court of the prince. I have been charged with the training and instruction of a group of unworldly young ladies, to teach them the pleasures of total subservience and to instruct them in the arts of sexual gratification. My task is complete. My lord, I present my angels of delight.'

She stepped to one side and clapped her hands. The heavy doors at the far end of the room swung open and the eight nervous girls entered, followed by eight handsome and naked young men. Each of the girls had a heavy chain drawn tightly about her waist, but was otherwise equally naked. They faced off in a line across the room and the males followed suit to stand one behind each of them. Sahria noticed with satisfaction that all the males sported an erection. They would need to, if the race were to be a success.

She turned to face the prince once more. 'My lord, I wish to present an event of my own design. I have promised the girls that, with your permission, whoever wins the race will be the first to enjoy your pleasure.'

The prince nodded and sat back in his throne to enjoy the spectacle.

Sahria clapped her hands again and the girls immediately dropped to a kneeling position on the marble floor. They moved forward and rested their hands in front of them so that their bottoms were presented to the eager gaze of the young men behind them. Then they too knelt and waited for Sahria's signal.

She clapped again and each of the young men eased his erection inside the girl before him. They then grasped the girls' thighs and struggled to their feet, holding the legs of their steeds around their hips. Some of them had a little difficulty with this manoeuvre, but eventually they all stood in a line with their cocks firmly embedded in the girls' juicy pussies.

Sahria turned to face the court. 'Should any of the young men slip from inside his steed,' she announced, 'they must both start the race again. Should any of the young men come before the race is won, they have lost and must leave the competition.' A number of people in the crowd laughed, and she saw that even the prince smiled.

She turned to face the line and paused for a moment. Then she clapped her hands and the race began. Jo-Jo and Su-Lee immediately fell forwards, having been pushed too hard by their riders. The four of them fell into a heap of tangled limbs and quickly struggled to regain their positions. Meanwhile, Agita's rider was clearly having difficulty with the voluptuous girl. He was a sturdy youth, but was weakening visibly. He staggered on nevertheless.

Mena and Aisha were leading the fray, no doubt due to their slightness of build. The twins, Shalma and Lisha, were close behind them, and they too were making good progress. Zia was last and, from the look on her rider's face, it seemed unlikely that he would finish the race.

Su-Lee and her rider were almost there, and Sarne was already clutching his erection in anticipation of impending delights. Su-Lee was staring at the monster with lust in her eyes. She was pulling herself furiously along the marble floor with her hands, and her rider was clearly having difficulty in remaining mounted. She reached out to grasp the prince's erection, and suddenly the young man's cock sprang from within her.

'Back to the start!' ordered Sahria.

Su-Lee looked desperately at her through tearful eyes, but the dejected pair disentangled themselves and scurried back to the start.

It was Aisha who was nearing the throne now. Having seen what had happened to Su-Lee she moved her hands carefully along the floor with measured paces. As she moved her bottom swayed from side to side and her rider was staring at the pert globes through lustful eyes. Sahria wondered if he would be able to hold back for just a few more seconds. She saw him look away from Aisha's delightful buttocks and his jaw tightened. He grasped her thighs tightly and forced her to stop, the expression on his face one of anguish. Mena and her rider were almost upon them. Aisha looked back and saw them, and begged her partner to move on.

The young man gritted his teeth and forced her to move quickly forward. Aisha reached out and grasped the prince's erection, and then fell to her knees triumphantly. Her rider sprang from her as she fell and he ejaculated immediately, sending a stream of sperm over her back. The onlookers cheered uproariously, but the race had been won.

Aisha rose to her feet and stood before the prince with her head bowed.

'Take your prize, young lady,' he encouraged.

She smiled, turned her back to him, and then sat on his lap. He slipped inside her with little difficulty, until Aisha had absorbed the full length, and the onlookers murmured their approval.

The other girls had dislodged themselves from their riders and watched enviously as Aisha ground up and down on her prize, her expression a picture of sheer bliss. Such was the intensity of her pleasure that she didn't last long, and with her eyes clamped tightly shut, her cheeks flushed, and a husky sigh, she shuddered to a long and exhausting orgasm.

Prince Sarne smiled as Aisha flopped like rag-doll back against his broad chest. He looked up at Sahria. 'You have done well, princess of pleasure,' he said warmly. 'You have amused me. That was quite the best entertainment that I have seen in many a year. Come to my rooms later, and we will talk.'

Princess Sahria stood at the arched window of the bedroom. She gazed at the lush fields and the distant mountains and felt very proud. She turned to face the room. Prince Sarne, her husband, lay asleep on the large bed. His cock lay limply across his muscular stomach, and her sex pulsed as she remembered the delights of the previous night – their wedding night.

She turned and looked out into the distance again. The kingdom was beautiful and, above all, it was her kingdom.

Exciting titles available from Chimera

* * *

All **Chimera** titles are/will be available from your local bookshop or newsagent, or direct from our mail order department. Please send your order with a cheque or postal order (made payable to *Chimera Publishing Ltd*) to: **Chimera Publishing Ltd., PO Box 152, Waterlooville, Hants, PO8 9FS.** If you would prefer to pay by credit card, email us at: **chimera@fdn.co.uk** or call our **24 hour telephone/fax credit card hotline: +44 (0)23 92 783037** (Visa, Mastercard, Switch, JCB and Solo only).

To order, send: Title, author, ISBN number and price for each book ordered, your full name and address, cheque or postal order for the total amount, and include the following for postage and packing:

UK and BFPO: £1.00 for the first book, and 50p for each additional book to a maximum of £3.50.

Overseas and Eire: £2.00 for the first book, £1.00 for the second and 50p for each additional book.

*Titles £5.99. All others £4.99

For a copy of our free catalogue please write to:

Chimera Publishing Ltd
Readers' Services
PO Box 152
Waterlooville
Hants
PO8 9FS

Or visit our Website for details of all our superb titles and secure ordering
www.chimerabooks.co.uk

Beamish Museum | TURN LEFT
AT ROUNDAB

07855
320109